龙脊沧桑话保定

讲述长城故事

李会斌 主编
韩红梅 译

The Vicissitudes of the Great Wall in Baoding

Telling the Stories of the Great Wall

河北大学出版社
·保定·

出 版 人：朱文富
责任编辑：李 达
助理编辑：冯喆圆
装帧设计：赵 谦
责任校对：兰彩红
责任印制：闻 利

图书在版编目（CIP）数据

龙脊沧桑话保定 ：讲述长城故事 / 李会斌主编 ；韩红梅译 . -- 保定 ：河北大学出版社，2020.12
ISBN 978-7-5666-1796-5

Ⅰ . ①龙… Ⅱ . ①李… ②韩… Ⅲ . ①新闻报道－作品集－中国－当代 Ⅳ . ① I253

中国版本图书馆 CIP 数据核字（2021）第 005511 号

LONGJI CANGSANG HUA BAODING
JIANGSHU CHANGCHENG GUSHI

出版发行：河北大学出版社
地址：河北省保定市七一东路2666号 邮编：071000
电话：0312-5073019 0312-5073029
网址：www.hbdxcbs.com
邮箱：hbdxcbs818@163.com
印 刷：保定市正大印刷有限公司
幅面尺寸：145 mm×210 mm
字 数：165千字
印 张：7
版 次：2020年12月第1版
印 次：2020年12月第1次印刷
书 号：ISBN 978-7-5666-1796-5
定 价：48.00 元

编委会

总策划 杨宝东

策　划 陈　伟　耿彦瑞

主　编 李会斌

副主编 席晓靖　张　强　单　娜

编　委 周　丹　吴超才　韩　朝

行走龙脊间　书写长城魂（序）

2019年8月，习近平总书记在甘肃考察时强调：“长城凝聚了中华民族自强不息的奋斗精神和众志成城、坚韧不屈的爱国情怀，已经成为中华民族的代表性符号和中华文明的重要象征。要做好长城文化价值发掘和文物遗产传承保护工作，弘扬民族精神，为实现中华民族伟大复兴的中国梦凝聚起磅礴力量。”

同年12月，中央全面深化改革委员会审议通过的《长城、大运河、长征国家文化公园建设方案》正式印发，河北段长城被纳入重点建设范围，其中，就包括保定长城。

如何响应总书记的号召？如何落实国家的建设方案？如何将保定长城独特的魅力和历史文化，推向全国、全世界？保定日报社积极筹划，“弘扬历史文化　讲述长城故事”大型系列宣传报道活动由此展开。

这是一组经过认真调研后精心策划的系列报道。保定日报社组织骨干记者组成报道组，报道前，专门组织召开多次座谈会，实地调研，并邀请权威专家全程指导。同时，广泛听取文化界人士、广大读者意见，确定报道主线和报道标准。在报道形式上，作为保定日报社融媒体改革重点实践项目之一，该系列报道采取了文字、图片、长短视频结合的方式，每一篇报道力求文字精致、图片恢宏、视频优美。《保定日报》《保定晚报》及《保定日报》官方微信、《保定晚报》官方微信、掌握保定手机客户端、抖音、快手等多平台集中发布报道，融媒体传播推广效果明显。

这是一组内容丰富的报道。划分了中国游牧文明和农业文明的保定长城，修建历史跨度达1954年。著名的“内三关”（居庸关、紫荆关、倒马关）中的紫荆关、倒马关坐落在保定境内。保定更是全中国和全世界唯一集合了山地长城、平原河堤长城、平原地下长城和水系长城的地区。涞源县120公里明长城全线均被列入全国重点文物保护单位，这在全国是唯一的。保定长城沿线是晋察冀抗日根据地核心区域和指挥机关所在，是八路军发动的百团大战的重要战场。本系列报道，先从宏观出发，再从不同地域着手，将长城故事娓娓道来，历史故事与现存状况相结合，既有历史意义又有现实意义。

这是一组践行“四力”的报道。报道方案出台后，报道组分赴涞源、易县、阜平、唐县等众多县域，跋山涉水现场采访，甚至在雪后冒着危险爬到山顶采访。其间，被树枝划伤，在山坡上摔倒，忍饥挨饿采访成为常态，极大地锻炼了采访队伍。

稿件见报后，引发了强烈的社会反响。学习强国平台及澎湃新闻、新浪网、搜狐网、腾讯网等重要网站纷纷转载，今日头条、抖音、快手、华人头条等众多新媒体平台纷纷播发，省、市、县众多微信公众号先后转载转发，形成“镇版刷屏”之效，引发现象级传播，引起全社会对保定长城的关注。

为了向全世界宣传、推介保定长城，本书采用中英文对照的方式，主译者为韩红梅，参译者有杜盼盼、王晶、孔亚萌、张青青、杨星星。

Walking along the "Dragon Backbone" Recounting the Great Wall Stories (Preface)

In August 2019, General Secretary Xi Jinping emphasized during an inspection in Gansu Province, "the Great Wall embodies the national spirit of self-improvement and patriotic sentiment of unity and perseverance. It has become a representative sign of the Chinese nation and a significant symbol of Chinese civilization. We should do well in exploring the cultural value of the Great Wall, and inheriting and protecting cultural relics and heritage, and then carry forward the national spirit and pool mighty strength for realizing the Chinese dream of national rejuvenation."

In December of the same year, the Great Wall, The Grand Canal and the Long March National Cultural Park, which were reviewed and approved by the central committee for deepening overall reform, were officially issued, and the Hebei section of the Great Wall was included in the scope of key construction projects, including the Baoding Great Wall.

How to respond to the call of the General Secretary? How to implement the country's construction plan? How to present the unique charm and historical culture of the Baoding Great Wall to the country and the world? *Baoding Daily* actively planned a series of large-scale publicity campaigns—Promoting History and Culture and Telling Great Wall Stories.

This is a series of reports elaborately planned after careful investigation. Before the reports were released, key journalists of Baoding Daily organized a report team. They held seminars, conducted on-the-spot investigations, and invited experts to guide the whole process. Meanwhile, they widely listened to opinions from cultural circles and readers, to determine the mainline and standards of the coverage. In the form of reporting, as one of the key practice projects of *Baoding Daily*'s convergence media reform, this series of reports adopts a combination of text, pictures, and short and long videos, with each report striving for exquisite text, magnificent pictures, and beautiful videos. The reports are released on *Baoding Daily*, *Baoding Evening News*, their official WeChat accounts, Knowing Baoding app, TikTok, Kwai, and other platforms, the promotion effects of which are outstanding.

This is a rich and magnificent report. The Baoding Great Wall, which divided the nomadic civilization and agricultural civilization in China, was built in 1954. Among famous "Inner Three Passes"(Juyongguan, Zijingguan and Daomaguan), Zijingguan and Daomaguan are located in Baoding. Baoding is the only area that gathers mountain great wall, plain river embankment great wall, plain underground great wall and drainage great wall in China and the world. The whole section of the Ming Great Wall in Laiyuan, stretching 120 kilometers, are listed as one of the national key cultural relics protection units, which is the only one in the country. Along the Baoding Great Wall is the core area and command post of Jin-Cha-Ji Anti-Japanese Military Base, and the main battlefield of the "Hundred Regiment War" launched by the Eighth Route Army. The series of reports, starting from the macro perspective, and then focusing on different regions, present stories of the Great Wall in detail. The combination of historical stories and existing status has both historical and practical significance.

This series of reports practices the "Four Abilities". After the introduction of the reporting plan, the reporting team went to Laiyuan, Yixian, Fuping, Tangxian, and many other counties, trekking through the mountains to cover the scene, and even risked climbing to the mountain top after the snow. During the reporting, being cut by branches, falling on the slope, and suffering starvation for interviews became the norm, which greatly exercised the interview team.

The reports triggered a strong social reaction after release, and have been reprinted or broadcast by Xuexi Qiangguo, important news websites like ThePaper, Sina.com, Sohu.com, and QQ.com, new-media platforms like TouTiao, TikTok, Kwai, and Chinese Headline New Media, as well as WeChat official accounts of various provinces, cities, and counties. The spread of the reports was phenomenal, attracting the whole country to pay attention to the Great Wall in Baoding.

In order to publicize the Baoding Great Wall to the world, this book is written in Chinese and English. The main translator is Han Hongmei, and the co-translators are Du Panpan, Wang Jing, Kong Yameng, Zhang Qingqing and Yang Xingxing.

目 录

CONTENTS

龙脊沧桑话保定（上）

李慧英　苑永涛

赵成侯六年（前369），中山筑长城。保定境内中山长城，填补古长城调研空白。上下两千年，纵横十万里。

初冬暖阳里，李文龙教授伏案桌前整理资料，看着那一段段文字、一张张照片，心向往之。边风瑟瑟的崇山峻岭间，是他最痴迷的保定古长城。作为一名长城调查研究者，33年来，河北大

战国中山长城唐县风山庄段

学博物馆副馆长李文龙走遍了河北省内各个长城遗址，并参与了《河北省志·长城志》《中国文物地图集·河北分册》等重要著作的编纂工作。

长城，俯卧在祖国大地的巨龙，翻越巍巍群山，穿过茫茫草原，跨越浩瀚沙漠，奔向辽阔大海。作为古代社会最宏伟、持续修筑时间最长、最系统的军事防御工程，长城见证了中华民族2000余年的生存、进化、发展史。保定古长城，更如同一本厚重的史书，等待人们捧读。

保定，地处辽阔的华北平原中部，在历史上是战争频发之地。从炎黄时代起便有多个民族长期生活于此，《易经》就曾记载："王公设险，以守其国。"所以，自古以来保定就是修建长城的重要地区。

"保定境内主要有中山长城、燕南长城及明长城，现存明朝以前长城墙体约225公里，明长城墙体约193公里。其历史延续之长、建筑类型之多样、防御体系之严密，在河北古代长城中占有极其重要的位置。尤其在明朝，保定作为京畿重地，长城的修筑更是达到了高峰。"李文龙教授娓娓道来。

随着李文龙教授的讲述，翻开长城这本史书，时光追溯至公元前369年。战国时期，"千乘之国"中山国位于燕国、赵国之间，主要活动区域在今石家庄中部、北部，保定南部。中山国多次与燕国、赵国发生战争，所以修筑长城御敌。经过多方的佐证，李文龙教授得出结论：中山国是河北境内最先修筑长城的诸侯国。

然而，关于战国中山长城的调查研究，始终停留在《史记·赵世家》：赵成侯六年（前369），中山筑长城。除此之外，没有任何依据可循。直至保定境内中山长城被人们发现，才填补了这一空白。

1988年，考古工作者在唐县唐河东岸发现一个石砌长城遗迹，之后数年又陆续在曲阳县、顺平县、涞源县发现相近的长城遗迹，经查证确定为战国中山长城。中山长城由涞源县黄土岭村开始，沿唐河东岸大致呈南北走向延伸，最终止于唐县灌城村，已发现约89公里。此外，顺平县隘门口、曲阳县郑家庄王快水库北侧的山岭上也发现了长城遗存。长城沿线还发现4处城址、2处屯戍遗址及6处烽燧遗址。中山长城以主干城墙为主体，另在一些险要的关口筑城或筑墙扼守，在城墙内侧修筑较大的城址为屯戍点，或在城墙附近驻兵防守，共同构成一道严密的防御体系。长城墙体为石砌或土石混砌，残宽1—2.5米，残高0.4—3米。

保定境内明朝之前的长城遗存，除了中山长城，还有沿南易水河而建的燕南长城，又称“易水长城”。战国时期，燕昭王即位后，励精图治，招贤纳士，燕国进入最强盛期。名将乐毅南伐强齐，秦开北破东胡，燕国开始向东北开拓。在此前后，燕国开始修筑南、北两道长城。

李文龙教授介绍，燕南长城位于保定、廊坊境内的易县、徐水、容城、安新、雄县、文安、大城七县，总长约259公里。保定境内的燕南长城长约136公里，首起于易县西南30公里的太和庄西侧的狼窝尖山，沿南易水河北岸延伸，进入徐水后继续沿瀑河（南易水河下游）北岸东行至遂城西。长城跨瀑河，向东经徐水入容城、安新，沿白洋淀北堤转北、转东而行。进入雄县后跨越大清河，沿河北岸进入廊坊市文安县。燕南长城的墙体有土石混砌和黄土夯筑两种形制，基宽4—15米，顶宽1—4米，存高1—6.3米。燕南长城许多地段利用古代堤防为墙体，兼具防水、防御双重功能，这也再次体现了古人的智慧。

龙脊沧桑，千年未绝，历史的车轮裹挟着朝代更迭滚滚向前，古城保定那金戈铁马、烽火连天的岁月被垒叠在一块块青砖之上，但长城的修筑并未停止，人们借助长城保家卫国的勇气及不屈不挠的民族精神仍在延续。

（历史文化顾问：河北大学博物馆副馆长、教授李文龙；直隶总督署博物馆吴蔚）

The Vicissitudes of the Great Wall in Baoding (I)

Li Huiying Yuan Yongtao

"In the sixth year of Emperor Chenghou of Zhao State during the Warring States Period, the Great Wall was built in Zhongshan State." The Zhongshan Great Wall in Baoding fills the gap in the research on the ancient Great Wall. Stretching for a hundred thousand Li, the Great Wall spans a history of 2, 000 years.

Basking in the warm sunshine of early winter, Professor Li Wenlong sorted out the documents at his desk. Looking at the sections of texts and photographs, he was deeply fascinated by the beautiful scenery. Among the lofty mountains and steep cliffs where the wind rustles, the ancient Great Wall in Baoding is the place he is most obsessed with. As a researcher and investigator of the Great Wall for 33 years, Li Wenlong, deputy curator of Hebei University Museum, has left his footprints all over the ancient Great Wall sites in Hebei Province. He also participated in the compilation of important works such as *Hebei Provincial Annals: Great Wall Volume* and *An Atlas of Chinese Cultural Relics: Hebei Volume.*

The Great Wall, a giant dragon lying prone on the motherland, winds over the lofty mountains, boundless grasslands and vast desert, and finally to the endless sea. As the most magnificent and systematic military defense project with the longest-lasting construction time in ancient times, the Great Wall has witnessed the history of survival, evolution and development of the

Chinese nation for more than two thousand years. The ancient Great Wall in Baoding is more like a thick history book, waiting for people to read.

Baoding, located in the middle of the vast North China Plain, is a place where wars were frequent. Many ethnic groups lived here for a long time since the Yan and Huang Era(primitive society period). As recorded in *The Book of Changes*, "The emperors set up steep passes to defend their country." Therefore, Baoding has been a vital area for the construction of the Great Wall since ancient times.

"There are mainly the Zhongshan Great Wall, the Yannan Great Wall(in the south of Yan State)and the Ming Great Wall in Baoding. The existing ramparts of the Great Wall built before the Ming Dynasty are about 225 kilometers long, and those ramparts built during the Ming Dynasty are about 193 kilometers long. With its long history, diverse construction types and tight defense system, the Great Wall in Baoding occupies an extremely important position in the ancient Great Wall of Hebei Province. Especially in the Ming Dynasty, the construction of the Great Wall in Baoding reached its peak for its short distance to the capital." Professor Li Wenlong said.

With the narration of Professor Li Wenlong, we opened the history book of the Great Wall, dating back to 369 BC During the Warring States Period, Zhongshan States, "a state with a thousand chariots", was located between Yan and Zhao States. Its central area was in the middle and north of Shijiazhuang and the south of Baoding. The Zhongshan State fought wars frequently with Yan and Zhao States, so the Great Wall was built to resist the enemy. After collecting a variety of evidences, Professor Li Wenlong concluded that Zhongshan State was the first vassal state which initiated the construction work of the Great Wall in Hebei Province.

However, the investigation and research on the Zhongshan Great Wall in the Warring States Period always stay in the *Historical Records of Zhao Family*, In the sixth year of Zhao Chenghou(the emperor of the Zhao State during the Warring States Period)in 369 BC, the Great Wall was built in Zhongshan State. However, there is no other evidence for this. It was not until the Zhongshan Great Wall in Baoding was discovered that this gap was filled.

In 1988, archaeologists discovered the relics of a stone-built Great Wall on the east bank of the Tang River in Tangxian County. In the following years, similar relics of the Great Wall were discovered in Quyang, Shunping, and Laiyuan County, which were confirmed to be the Great Wall of Zhongshan State during the Warring States Period. The Zhongshan Great Wall starts from Huangtuling Village in Laiyuan County, extends from north to south along the east bank of the Tang River, and ends at Guancheng village of Tangxian County. The section that has been found is about 89 miles long. In addition, the relics of the Great Wall were also discovered in the mountains at Aimenkou Village of Shunping County and on the north side of Wangkuai Reservoir at Zhengjia Village of Quyang County. Four city sites, two garrison sites and six beacon sites were found along the Great Wall. The Zhongshan Great Wall formed a tight defense system with the main wall as the main body, some vital passes or walls built to guard the wall, larger city sites built on the inside of the ramparts as garrison points, or stationed troops near the wall for defense. All of these jointly constitute an elaborate defense system. The walls of the ancient Great Wall are made of stone, or mixture of soil and stone, with a residual width of 1 to 2.5 meters and a residual height of 0.4 to 3 meters.

The relics of the Great Wall in Baoding before the Ming Dynasty include the Zhongshan Great Wall, and the Yannan Great Wall along the south Yishui River, also known as the "Yishui Great Wall". During the Warring States Period, after Ji Zhi(the Emperor of Yan State)ascended the throne, he made great efforts to govern the country and recruit talents. Therefore, the Yan State entered its prime time. Yue Yi, a famous general of Yan State, led armed forces to suppress the powerful Qi State. Qin Kai defeated the people in Donghu(the ancient nomads in northeast China). From then on, Yan State began to expand to the northeast. Around this time, the southern and northern sections of the Great Wall started to be constructed .

Professor Li wenlong introduced that the Yannan Great Wall was located in Baoding city, Xiong'an New Area and Langfang city, involving seven counties, namely Yixian, Xushui, Rongcheng, Anxin, Xiongxian, Wen'an and Dacheng. Its total length is about 259 miles. The Yannan Great Wall in Baoding is about 136 kilometers long. It starts at Langwojian Mountain on the west side of Taihe Town, 30 kilometers southwest of Yixian. It extends along the north bank of the Nanyishui River, flows eastward through Yixian along the north bank of the Puhe River(downstream of the Nanyishui River) to the west of Suicheng Town. The Great Wall crosses the Puhe River, flows eastward through Xushui, enters Rongcheng and Anxin, and then turns north and east along the north bank of Baiyangdian Lake. After entering Xiongxian, it crosses the Daqing River and enters Wen'an of Langfang City along the north bank of the river. The ramparts of the Yannan Great Wall have different building materials: one is made of stone and soil; the other is made of rammed loess. The width of its base is 4 to 15 meters, the width of its top is 1 to 4 meters, and the residue height is 1 to 6.3 meters. Many sections of the Yannan Great Wall use ancient dikes as walls, which have the dual functions of waterproofing and defense. This manifests the great wisdom of the ancient people.

The majestic Great Wall have endured for thousands of years, and the wheel of history is rolling forward with the change of dynasties. A piece of black brick in Baoding carries the memory of the years when soldiers defended invaders during the war. The construction of the Great Wall has been continuing, and people's courage and indomitable national spirit to defend their country with the help of the Great Wall are spreading.

(The consultant on history and culture: Professor Li Wenlong, deputy curator of Hebei University Museum; Wu Wei, staff member of Zhili Governor' s Office Museum)

战国中山长城
唐县万里段

龙脊沧桑话保定（中）

李慧英　孟海英　吴战平　王栋

因地形，用险制塞，历来战事频仍。保定明长城，拱卫京畿的最后一道屏障。

登上长城，才能真正体会古人据险以守的智慧。

冬日的紫荆关长城显得越发苍劲，虽不如当年严整，却仍不失威武气势。指着大城套小城、酷似一朵梅花形状的关城，易县文物保管所所长李连柱语气豪迈：“紫荆关有‘畿南第一雄关’之称，为明长城九大名关之一，自古以来就是华北平原的重要门户，是兵家必争之地，曾经历大小战斗140多次。”

顺着李连柱的目光远远望去，流动在山脊上的长城墙体，按照山体的走势变换着节奏，呈现出优美的曲线变化。墙体高低宽窄随地形的险要形势而异，山高地险处的墙体相对低窄，平地要冲之处墙体则高大宽阔，墙体与关堡、隘口、烽火台等军事防御设施一起，共同组成完整的防御体系。这，正是明长城的显著特征。

横亘于中国北方辽阔地域的明长城，是举世公认的古代世界规模最大、持续修筑时间最长的军事防御工程，是中国封建社会

北楼台

工程技术水平和劳动人民聪明智慧的集中体现。在保定境内，巍峨雄伟的明长城绵延长达193公里，至今仍保存着一大批具有代表性的雄关要塞。

“明王朝为了加强京城的防御能力，在万里长城的主线之内，在北京西北部、保定和山西境内修筑了一条与之相连的内长城，构成守卫京城的最后一道防线。而重中之重的‘内三关’，更是有两关地处保定境内。”河北大学博物馆副馆长李文龙寥寥数语，道破保定明长城至关重要的军事价值及战略地位。

经过无数次的实地走访和考证，考古学出身的李文龙教授终于掌握了保定明长城的基本情况。保定明长城史称“内长城”，明朝时叫“次边”，属于真保镇（总兵驻保定，管辖的长城全长390公里，北起紫荆关，经倒马关、龙泉关、娘子关，南至故关）管辖。长城由张家口市涿鹿县马水口南入涞水县，大部分地段以

涞源白石口长城

山为险未筑墙。长城向西南入涞源县，沿东北向西南走向横跨涞源县全境，入山西省灵丘县，由灵丘县再入阜平县，南转西抵吴王口。由此分为两支：一支向西北又入灵丘县；一支向西南沿河北、山西两省交界南行，进入灵寿县、平山县、井陉县。保定明长城一是有边墙的，沿涞源县东北而走；一是无边墙而以数所关口、楼台相连的，自涞源县西南端至阜平县境内，均为石砌。长城墙体总长约193公里，包括关城26座、敌台344座、烽火台131座，著名关隘有紫荆关、倒马关和龙泉关。

长城虽然历经战火硝烟及数百年的风雨剥蚀，很多地方已经坍塌，其砖石结构、敌台等更是所剩不多，但看那陡峭的山脊上用巨大石块砌成的墙体，依然可以想见其当初的雄伟与坚固。

因地形，用险制塞的保定明长城，历来战事频仍。李文龙讲述，明清时期，保定长城沿线紫荆关、倒马关、龙泉关、插箭岭、乌龙沟、浮图峪等重要关隘为守卫京城而多次发生战事。在烽火连天的抗日战争时期，长城沿线更是八路军和日寇反复争夺的重点地区之一。虽然在现代战争条件下，长城的防御功能减弱了，但是各大关口都属于交通要塞，战略意义重大。八路军在长城内外与日寇展开殊死搏斗，留下长城抗战的铁血烙印，大龙华战斗、黄土岭战斗、东团堡战斗、雁宿崖战斗等著名战事都发生于此。其中，1939年的黄土岭战斗歼敌900余人，并击毙日军素有“名将之花”之称的中将指挥官阿部规秀，创造了我军抗战史上的辉煌战例，在当时极大地振奋了中国军民的抗日信心。

蓝天白云下，雄关文脉长。古长城沧桑古朴，残旧的墙壁无声地诉说着当年的狼烟滚滚。脚下的台阶并不平整，风吹雨打

涞源碾子沟长城

涞源碾子沟长城

的痕迹依稀可见。每一级台阶都记录着战火纷飞与硝烟弥漫的岁月，越过古地图中那些残缺不全的墨迹，在这里，我们与真实的长城相遇。

（历史文化顾问：河北大学博物馆副馆长、教授李文龙；直隶总督署博物馆吴蔚）

The Vicissitudes of the Great Wall in Baoding (II)

Li Huiying Meng Haiying Wu Zhanping Wang Dong

Although forts were built on steep terrain, battles were still frequent all along. The Ming Great Wall in Baoding was the last shield of the capital city.

One cannot really understand the wisdom of "fortifying on steep terrain for sake of defense" of ancestors until he mounts onto the Great Wall.

In winter, Zijingguan of the Great Wall looks more solemn. Although neat formation is weakened than the past, its mighty vigor remains. Pointing at the pass city, a city encircled in a bigger city shaped like a plum blossom, Li Lianzhu, Director of Cultural Relics Protection Institute of Yixian County, could not hold back his pride, "Zijingguan, known as 'No.1 Impregnable Pass of Jinan', is one of the nine famous passes of the Ming Great Wall. Since ancient times, it has been an important gateway to the North China Plain and a hotly contested spot. It witnessed more than 140 battles, big or small."

The Great Wall adapts itself to the fluctuations of the mountain massif. A graceful curve is visible. The dimension of the rampart also varies with the changing terrain it is lower and narrower in steep areas, while higher and wider in flat areas. The ramparts, together with forts, passes, beacon towers and other defense works, constitute a complete defense system. This is exactly the marked feature of the Ming Great Wall.

The Ming Great Wall, which stretches across the vast area of northern

China, is regarded as the largest military defense project with the longest duration of construction in ancient time. It is the embodiment of the engineering technology and the wisdom of the working people in China's feudal society. In Baoding, the majestic Ming Great Wall stretches for 193 kilometers, and a large number of representative passes and fortresses are still well-preserved.

"In order to strengthen the defense capability of the capital, the Ming Dynasty built an Inner Great Wall in the northwest of Beijing, Baoding and Shanxi within the main line of the Great Wall, forming the last line of defense for the capital. The most important Three Inner Passes are Juyongguan, Zijingguan and Daomaguan, and two of them are located in Baoding." Li Wenlong, deputy curator of Hebei University Museum, talked briefly about the important military value and strategic position of the Ming Great Wall in Baoding.

After countless field visits and textual research, Professor Li Wenlong, who specialize in archaeology, mastered the basic situation of the Ming Great Wall in Baoding. The Ming Great Wall in Baoding was called "the Inner Great Wall" in history and "Secondary Frontier" in the Ming Dynasty. It was under the jurisdiction of Zhenbao town(the commander-in-chief was stationed in Baoding. With the total length of 390 kilometers, it starts from Zijingguan in the north, passes through Daomaguan, Longquanguan, Niangziguan, and ends at Guguan in the south). The Great Wall runs from Mashuikou Pass in Zhuolu County of Zhangjiakou City to the south of Laishui County. No city wall was built in the majority of this section because the high mountains in there could be used as barriers. The Great Wall enters Laiyuan County to the southwest, crosses the whole territory of Laiyuan County, and then enters Lingqiu County of Shanxi Province. Then, it enters Fuping County from Lingqiu County, and then it turns from south to the west and arrives at Wuwangkou Pass. It is divided into two branches: one goes northwest and enters Lingqiu County; the other goes southwest along the junction of Hebei and Shanxi Provinces, and enters Lingshou County, Pingshan County, and Jingxing County. One section of the Ming Great Wall in Baoding has flank walls along the northeast of Laiyuan County. Another section has no flank walls along the southwest end of Laiyuan County to Fuping County. It is connected by stone-made passes and towers. The total length of the Great Wall in Baoding is about 193 kilometers. There are 26 pass cities, 344 watchtowers, and 131 beacon towers. The famous passes include Zijingguan, Daomaguan and Longquanguan.

Although the Great Wall has suffered collapses, and damaged masonry structure and watchtowers due to the flames of war and wind and rain erosion in hundreds of years, one can still imagine its original majesty and solidity when looking at the walls constructed with huge rocks on the steep ridge.

The Ming Great Wall in Baoding, built according to the terrain and used to control the vital passes, has always been a place where frequent wars occurred in history. Li Wenlong recounted that during the Ming and Qing Dynasties, many wars for defending the capital took place in vital passes along the Great Wall in Baoding, such as Zijingguan, Daomaguan, Longquanguan, Chajianling, Wulonggou, and Futuyu. During the Anti-Japanese war, the territory along the Great Wall was one of the key areas which the Eighth Route Army and the Japanese invaders repeatedly fought for. Although the defensive function of the Great Wall is weakened due to modern warfare, all the major passes are traffic fortresses with great strategic significance. The Eighth Route Army fought desperately against the Japanese invaders inside and outside the Great Wall, leaving behind the indelible marks of blood and weapons on the Great Wall. A number of well-known battles took place here, including Dalonghua Battle, Huangtuling Battle, Dongtuanbao Battle, and Yansuya Battle. Among them, more than 900 enemy troops were wiped out. Japanese General Commander Abu Guixiu, titled as "A Stor of Generals", was killed in Huangtuling Battle. It was a great victory of our army in the history of Anti-Japanese War, which invigorated the confidence of Chinese soldiers and civilians in resisting Japanese invaders at that time.

Under the blue sky and white clouds, the impregnable pass has its cultural context continued. The ancient Great Wall is a witness of vicissitudes. The klunky walls silently tell the story of beacon-fire in history. The steps are not smooth, and traces of wind and rain are faintly visible. Each step records those years of wars. Through the incomplete marks in an ancient map, we meet the real Great Wall here.

(The consultant on history and culture: Professor Li Wenlong, deputy curator of Hebei University Museum; Wu Wei, staff member of Zhili Governor's Office Museum)

白石口长城

龙脊沧桑话保定（下）

李会斌　丁咏静　李慧英　赵顺利　吴战平

烽火长城，英雄保定。捍卫有形万里长城，筑牢无形精神长城。

青龙一经起群岭，尽是血肉筑平安。

长城，是一首律动的史诗。人们用脚步去丈量长城之长，用内心来表达长城之重。“汉家锁钥惟玄塞，隘地旌旗见紫

荆山口长城

荆。”“单于痛哭倒马关，羯奴半死飞狐道。”……热血保定，不乏文人墨客与诗词歌赋，景点故事与民间传说，凡此种种，用跨越时空的存在，展示长城文化的亘古长存。

2019年8月，习近平总书记在甘肃考察时强调：“长城凝聚了中华民族自强不息的奋斗精神和众志成城、坚韧不屈的爱国情怀，已经成为中华民族的代表性符号和中华文明的重要象征。要做好长城文化价值发掘和文物遗产传承保护工作，弘扬民族精神，为实现中华民族伟大复兴的中国梦凝聚起磅礴力量。”

捍卫有形万里长城，筑牢无形精神长城。万里中华魂，屹立永不倒。

“紫荆关头昼吹角，杀气军声满幽朔。”明朝诗人李梦阳用一首《石将军战场歌》，将自己对国家民族命运的深深忧患展现得淋漓尽致；清朝诗人严遂成在《龙泉关》中，用“燕晋分疆处，雄关控上游”等名句描写了龙泉关据险以守的地理优势；保定籍著名词作家阎肃创作的一曲《长城长》，更是写尽长城万古雄风……千百年来，借保定长城歌颂爱国情怀和英雄气概的诗词歌赋绵绵不断，彰显着民族之魂的血脉激荡与精神激昂。

相传宋朝大将杨延昭与辽军在倒马关激战，辽军渐处下风，于是答应以射箭划界。杨延昭落箭之地，就是辽军退后之所。结果，杨延昭一箭飞出30余里落下，就有了后来的涞源县插箭岭……这些地域性传说，并未淹没在历史烟云中，而是形成了一种地域文化，丰富着保定长城的人文情趣。借此典故，《不到长城非好汉》《塞上风云》《卫士》《八路军在长城上行进》《插箭岭战斗，八路军指挥所》《八路军收复插箭岭》等一批拍摄于

烟煤洞长城

保定长城的经典影视、摄影作品，再现英雄情怀。

长城所承载的文化精神，在不同历史时期，被赋予不同时代的生命与价值，为人们提供精神指引。保定，是一座英雄辈出的城市。抗战时期，为掩护主力部队与群众突围，投完最后一颗手榴弹，狼牙山五勇士决然跳下悬崖；涞源少年英雄王二小，不畏强敌，把日寇引进八路军伏击圈后壮烈牺牲；“太行山上新愚公”——河北农业大学教授李保国，35年如一日，扎根太行，用尽一生把科技和富裕带给农民；92岁的唐县老兵、老党员路维生，一心向党、一生为民，身后仍交最后一笔2万元党费，并捐献遗体……这，就是保定人民对长城精神的接续传承与生动诠释。

保护长城遗存，传承长城精神。保定，一直在行动。

“一定要把紫荆关保护好，不要让古老的紫荆关在我们这一代毁掉。”曾经指挥过著名的黄土岭战斗、大龙华战斗的开国上将杨成武于1987年、1992年来到紫荆关，对长城保护工作提出要求。自此，紫荆关开始了长达数十年的维修工程，这座著名的“紫塞金城”重现当年风骨。涞源县乌龙沟长城抢险保护工程，通过抢险加固和现状保护等修缮手段，解除了自然及人为因素对长城文物本体的破坏，最大限度地保留了长城自然、古朴的整体风貌。唐县倒马关关城城墙抢救性加固工程，使部分长城得到及时有效保护。2016年1月，保定市人民政府发布《关于做好全市区域内长城保护利用工作的通知》。2019年7月，保定市人大常委会召开长城保护地方立法立项论证会。目前，保定市宣传、文旅等部门和单位围绕申报长城文化公园项目的宣传保护、规划利用等方面工作已全面铺开。

涞源碾子沟长城

一段长城，情怀接力。涞源县烟煤洞乡唐子沟村，父亲李凤鸣从1988年开始义务巡查、守护村内明长城，儿子李勇2015年接替父亲，继续守护长城。数十年过去，村民们在扶贫搬迁中，相继告别世代居住的小山村，而李勇则一个人留下来，继续日复一日地巡护着古长城。像李凤鸣、李勇父子一样的长城守护员，还有很多，他们守护的是古长城，更是他们心中的长城。

长城保护，道阻且长。保护好身边的长城，才能筑牢人们心中的长城，才能让长城精神落地生根、拔节生长，深深融入保定人民的血脉之中，成为实现保定跨越崛起和复兴的强大精神力量。

The Vicissitudes of the Great Wall in Baoding (III)

Li Huibin Ding Yongjing Li Huiying Zhao Shunli Wu Zhanping

The fire once burnt on the beacon towers of the Great Wall, and heroes emerged in large numbers in Baoding. We should defend the tangible Great Wall and build the invisible spiritual Great Wall.

Once the green dragon rises it runs through mountains, and peace is guaranteed by flesh and blood.

The Great Wall, a rhythmic epic. People measure the length of the Great Wall with footsteps and express the weight of the Great Wall with hearts. "The Han ethnic group defends their home with the Great Wall, and the soldiers safeguard families at frontier fortresses." "The leader of Wassa cried bitterly at Daomaguan, because most of his soldiers died in Feihu Pass." For Baoding, there are many literati, poets, poetry, scenic spots and folklore, all of which exist in different times and space as an embodiment of the eternal existence of the Great Wall culture.

In August 2019, General Secretary Xi Jinping emphasized during an inspection in Gansu Province, "the Great Wall embodies the national spirit of self-improvement and patriotic sentiment of unity and perseverance. It has become a representative sign of the Chinese nation and a significant symbol of Chinese civilization. We should do well in exploring the cultural value of the Great Wall, and inheriting and protecting cultural relics and heritage, and then carry forward the national spirit and pool mighty strength for realizing the Chinese dream of national rejuvenation."

We need to defend the tangible Great Wall and build the invisible spiritual Great Wall. The Chinese soul of thousands of miles will stand and never fall.

"The horns were blown at Zijingguan during the day, the murderous atmosphere filled You-Shuo, and the sound of battle hit the sky", an excerpt from *A Song of General Shi at Battlefield* written by Li Mengyang, a poet of the Ming dynasty to show his deep concern for the nation's fate. In the Longquanguan, the poet Yan Suicheng of the Qing Dynasty depicted geographical advantage of Longquanguan in such famous sentences as "Where Yan and Jin borders lies an impregnable pass holding the upper reaches of the Yellow River"; The song *The Long Great Wall by Yan Su*, a well-known songwriter from Baoding, outlines the eternal glory of the Great Wall in even more details... For thousands of years, poems and songs on the Great Wall in Baoding are emerging ceaselessly, extolling patriotism and heroism, highlighting the enthusiasm and enterprising spirit of the nation.

Legend has it that in the fierce battle with general Yang Yanzhao of the Song Dynasty at Daomaguan, the Liao army gradually got disadvantaged and agreed with Yang to delimit the boundary by shooting an arrow and that the place where Yang Yanzhao's arrow fell was where the Liao army retreated. As a result, Yang Yanzhao's arrow fell down after flying more than 30 miles away at the place which was later called Chajianling, Laiyuan County... Such regional legends were not submerged in history, but formed a regional culture that enriches the cultural sentiment of the Baoding Great Wall. Based on these allusions, a batch of classic film and television works and photography works were shot on the Baoding Great Wall to reshape the heroic feelings, and the memorable years, such as *One Who Fails to Reach the Great Wall Is not a Hero, Storm on the Border, The Guardian, The Eighth Route Army Marching on the Great Wall, Chajianling Battle, the Eighth Route Army Command Post, The Eighth Route Army Recovers Chajianling...*

Baoding is a city that gives birth to a multitude of heroes. During the Anti-Japanese War, the five warriors of Langya Mountain, aiming to cover the main force and the masses to break through the siege and flee, determinedly jumped off the cliff after throwing the last grenade; Wang Erxiao, a young hero of Laiyuan, with no fear of the strong enemies, led the Japanese invaders into the Eighth Route Army's ambush and died a glorious death; "The New Foolish Old Man on Taihang Mountain"—Li Baoguo, a professor at Hebei Agricultural University, dedicated his entire life to bringing technology and prosperity to farmers for 35 years; Lu Weisheng, a 92-year-old veteran and party member of Tang County, devoted his life to the party and the people, still paid the last party fee of 20,000 yuan after death and donated his body... This is the continuous inheritance and vivid interpretation of the spirit of the Great Wall by the people of Baoding.

We need to protect the relics of the Great Wall and carry forward its spirit. Baoding has always been in action.

"We must ensure that Zijingguan is well protected and that the ancient pass is not destroyed by our generation." Yang Chengwu, a general who once commanded the well known Battles at Huangtuling and Dalonghua, came to Zijingguan in 1987 and 1992, and stressed the requirements for the protection of the Great Wall. Since then, a maintenance project of Zijingguan has been carried out for over a decade. Now, this famous "Purple Fort & Golden City"(Zi Sai Jin Cheng)reproduces its past vigor. The Great Wall rescue and protection project in Wulonggou, Laiyuan County has restored the damage caused by natural and human factors through emergency reinforcement, conservation of the current state and other means, preserving the natural and plain style of the Great Wall to the greatest extent. The city wall emergency reinforcement project of Daomaguan, Tangxian County has protected the Great Wall in a timely and effective manner. In January 2016, the Baoding municipal government issued the Notice on the Protection and Utilization of the Great Wall in the City; in July 2019, the Standing Committee of the Baoding Municipal People's Congress held a demonstration meeting on local legislation and project approval for the protection of the Great Wall; at present, Baoding municipal propaganda, cultural tourism and other departments and units are vigorously carrying out work around the publicity, protection, planning and utilization involving the application for the Great Wall Cultural Park project.

Guarding the Great Wall is a continuation of responsibility and patriotism. At Tangzigou Village of Yanmeidong Town, Laiyuan County,

Li Fengming began to voluntarily inspect and guard the Ming Great Wall in 1988. Then Li Yong, his son, continued to guard the Great Wall in 2015. Over the past few decades, in the process of poverty alleviation and relocation, villagers left the small mountain village where they have lived for generations, while Li Yong stayed alone and continued to patrol the ancient Great Wall day after day. There are many Great Wall protectors like Li Fengming and Li Yong. What they protect is not merely the ancient Great Wall, but the patriotic feelings rooted in their hearts as well.

It is an arduous and long journey to protect the Great Wall. Only by protecting the Great Wall around us can we firmly build the Great Wall in people's mind. As a result, the spirit of the Great Wall will take root, grow, and deeply integrate into the blood of Baoding people, and become a powerful spiritual force for the rise and rejuvenation of Baoding.

畿南第一雄　巍巍紫荆关

李会斌　丁咏静　李慧英　杨增红

阳光清透。这样的好天气，易县摄影爱好者杨增红必到紫荆关取景拍摄。俯仰之间，他通过镜头寻觅着曾经的黄尘古道、烽火边城，也感受着消逝的刀光剑影与鼓角争鸣。

紫荆关位于易县城西北45公里的紫荆岭上，始建于战国时期，距今2200多年。因当年漫山遍野的紫荆树，元朝始称紫荆关。明朝洪武初年，大兴土木改筑旧城再建新城，形成现今的规模，与居庸关、倒马关并称“内三关”。它西可扼控宣化、大同，东可直下居庸、燕京，为“畿南第一雄关”。这里地势险要，自古就是进入华北平原的重要门户之一，为兵家必争之地。

据《吕氏春秋》记载，紫荆关即“太行八陉”的第七陉“蒲阴陉”，秦汉时称“上谷关”，在东汉时又称“五阮关”，北魏时期，郦道元在《水经注》一书中称紫荆关为“子庄关”，宋、金时改称“金坡关”，是我国近千座关口中历史最为悠久的几座之一。

紫荆关关城周围最高海拔1080米，由5个大小不等的城圈组成，呈梅花状，城池方圆1万余平方米，建筑雄伟。沿拒马河南岸

紫塞金城

的800米城墙均为料石垒砌，全国独有。它不同于我国任何一处名关险塞的城池布局，而是根据地理环境，依山势而建，建筑布局独具匠心，作战时每个城圈可互为呼应，又可独立作战，自成防御体系，军事价值极高。

《方舆纪要》载：“易州控据西山，指顾代朔，东下则岐沟、督亢不可为固，西山则蜚狐雁门不足为险也。”明成祖迁都北京后，居庸关是抵御来自北方敌人侵扰的重要屏障。但事实证明，紫荆关在拱卫京城时具有居庸关不可替代的战略地位。明臣于谦曾说：“居庸、紫荆并为畿辅咽喉，论者尝先居庸，而后紫荆，不知寇窥居庸其得入者十之三，寇窥紫荆其得入者十之七……”南宋嘉定二年（1209），元太祖成吉思汗攻打居庸关，久攻不下，于是抽出主力南下，一举攻下紫荆关，在易县境内的五回岭大败金兵，又由长城内侧向外反攻居庸关，内外夹击，居庸关被攻破。

紫荆关长城与拒马河相映成趣

清朝，紫荆关已属腹地，但驻军兵额未减。康熙帝曾两次西巡，驻跸关城，检阅军校，南天门曾立有“天子阅武处”碑。直至近代，关城战火不断。《易县志》记载：“清光绪二十六年，八国联军据东高峰以大炮复攻关城……民国十五年，吴佩孚讨赤军战于紫荆关。”易县文物保管所所长李连柱说，据不完全统计，在紫荆关发生的战事有百余次。

长期自然侵蚀和历代战争，使紫荆关建筑布局遭到破坏，但关城还现存有城门3座、水门3座、水口29个、马道5条。专家调查发现，关城内存有古井、房基、磨盘等生活遗迹，实为一处完整的大遗址。

正是凭借重要的文物保护价值、军事研究价值和旅游观光价值，紫荆关于1996年被国务院列入全国重点文物保护单位。李连柱说，在杨成武将军等人的关心下，1992年紫荆关长城维修工程开始测绘设计，2003年施工，至2017年已累计投资2543万元，总计维修城墙2001米、城门3座、马道5条、水门2座。

昔日军事要塞，如今美景田园。紫荆关镇镇长张建军介绍，借助2016年9月首届河北省旅发大会，易县积极打造241省道紫荆关段风景大道，“油葵油菜花海”与“林下野花组合”装点出带动乡村旅游的景观廊道，并建成水上漂流项目，使经济效益、社会效益凸显。与此同时，周边农家乐发展到50余家。村民王会平不仅将农家乐经营得红红火火，还被推选为易县人大代表。

城门石刻“河山带砺”，仿若高擎的信念之炬。翻阅杨增红的帧帧图片，镜头下，紫荆关已经迈出由“兵家必争之地”向“游客向往之地”的铿锵步伐。

Zijingguan—No.1 Impregnable Pass of Jinan

Li Huibin Ding Yongjing Li Huiying Yang Zenghong

The sunshine was bright. On such fine days, Yang Zenghong, a photography enthusiast from Yixian County, must go to Zijingguan for scenery shooting. He tried to trace the past roads and border city via the lens, and meanwhile recalled the vanished blades, drums and horns.

Located on the Zijing Ridge, 45 kilometers northwest of Yixian County, Zijingguan was originally built in the Warring States Period, more than 2,200 years ago. Because of the Bauhinia trees all over the mountains, it got the name "Zijingguan" in the Yuan dynasty. In the early years of Hongwu Period in the Ming Dynasty, the old city was reconstructed. That was how today's layout came from. Zijingguan, Juyongguan and Daomaguan are collectively known as "Three Inner Passes". Zijingguan could control Xuanhua and Datong in the west, and lead to Juyong and Yanjing in the east, so it was called "No.1 Impregnable Pass of Jinan". On account of the precipitous terrain here, it has been one of the important gateways to the North China Plain since ancient times, and a hotly contested place for military commanders.

According to *Lv's Commentaries of History*, Zijingguan was the Puyin road, the seventh road of the so-called "Eight Routes at Taihang Mountain". It was also referred to as Shangguguan in the Qin and Han dynasties or as the Wuruanguan in the Eastern Han dynasty. During the Northern Wei period, Li Daoyuan referred to Zijingguan as the Zizhuangguan in his *Commentary on the Water Classic*; however, the name of the pass was changed to Jinpoguan during the Song and Jin dynasties. Among nearly 1,000 ancient passes in China, Zijingguan is one of the oldest passes.

The highest elevation of the surrounding city of Zijingguan is 1,080 meters. The city is comprised of 5 urban circles with varied sizes that are arranged in a pattern of plum blossom. Covering an area of about 10,000 square meters, the city accommodates quite magnificent architectural structures. Along the south bank of the Juma River is a rampart stretching 800 meters built entirely with squared stones, which is the only rampart of this kind in China. Differing from any other historically well-known passes and fortresses, the walls and moats in Zijingguan were arranged in accordance with geological conditions and adapted to the mountainous terrain. The architectural structures within the parameter of the pass were distributed in a uniquely ingenious way that enabled them not only to reciprocally support each other during war times, but each urban circle also functioned as an independent combat unit that had its own defense system, indicating an extremely high military value.

According to *Elaborations of the Essence of Geographical Treatises in the Histories*, "the Yi Prefecture exerts control over Xishan and immediate influences on Dai and Shuo Prefectures; to the east is Qigou and Dugang which are less impregnable while the Feihu and Yanmen Passes in the Xishan area are less precipitous". After Emperor Chengzu of the Ming Dynasty relocated the capital to Beijing, Juyongguan rose to be a major defense against invasion and harassment from northern enemies. However, it turned out that Zijingguan had occupied an irreplaceable strategic position in protecting the capital. "Both Juyongguan and Zijingguan passes are throats of the capital city and its environs. However, military commentators often put Juyongguan above Zijingguan, without knowing the fact that invaders are able to achieve 3 successes out of 10 attempts at Juyongguan but 7 successes out of 10 attempts at Zijingguan...", said Yu Qian, a famous military strategist of the Ming dynasty. In the second year of Jiading's rein in the Southern Song Dyansty(1209), Genghis Khan, Emperor Taizu of the Yuan Dynasty, attacked Juyongguan but without success over a long time. Thus, he diverted his main troops southwards and successfully took Zijingguan. His army defeated the Jin troops at Wuhuiling of Yixian County, and then turned back to attack Juyongguan from the southern side of the Great Wall. Having enemies in front and rear, Juyongguan was soon breached.

In the Qing Dynasty, the number of troops stationed in Zijingguan was not reduced despite the fact that it already resided inside the border of the country. In his two rounds of western inspection tours, Emperor Kangxi was stationed in Zijingguan where he inspected the military academy; at the Heavenly Southern Gate of the pass once stood a stone tablet which wrote "the Place where the Emperor Inspected His Army". Until the contemporary times, battles and wars had not been ceased around the pass city. According to records of the *Yixian Chronicles*, "in the 26th year of Guangxu's rein in the Qing dynasty, troops of the Eight Nation Allied Forces seized the eastern peak and attacked the pass using artillery... In the 15th year of the Republic of China, Wu Peifu launched a strike against the "red military forces" at Zijingguan." Li Lianzhu, director of the Cultural Relic Conservation Office of Yixian County, said that according to incomplete statistics, More than one hundred battles took place at Zijingguan.

Long-term natural erosion and historical wars have destroyed the layout of Zijingguan. However, there are still 3 city gates, 3 water gates, 29 water outlets, and 5 horse roads in Zijingguan city. Experts have discovered through investigations that there are ancient wells, building foundations, millstones and other living relics in Zijingguan, which is actually a large intact historical site.

Due to its important value in cultural relics protection, military research and tourism, Zijingguan was promulgated by the State Council as a national key Cultural Relics Protection Site in December 1996. Li Lianzhu said that under the care of General Yang Chengwu and others, The survey and design of the Maintenance Project of the Zijingguan Great Wall started in 1992, and the construction work began in 2003. By 2017, a total of RMB 25.43 million has been invested in the maintenance of 2,001 meters long city walls, 3 city gates, 5 horse roads, and 2 water gates.

What used to be a military fortress is now a beautiful countryside. Zhang Jianjun, mayor of Zijingguan Town, introduced that taking the chance brought about by the First Hebei Tourism Industrial Development Conference in September 2016, Yixian County has actively built the scenic avenue of Zijingguan section of Provincial Highway 241. The oil sunflowers, rape flowers, and different combinations of wildflowers have decorated the landscape corridor to drive rural tourism, and the rafting adventures there have further created economic and social benefits. Up to now, there are more than 50 agritainment activity holders in the surrounding area, among whom Wang Huiping, a villager, not only runs his hotel into the ground, but also was elected as a representative of the People's Congress of Yixian County.

The stone inscriptions on the city gate, which writes "He Shan Dai Li (meaning one's resolution will not be even the slightest shaken over time)", is like a torch of faith. Looking through every photo taken by Yang Zenghong, we may clearly see that Zijingguan has been transformed changed from "a must for military strategists" into "a land for tourists".

飞狐古道苍龙起　烽火连天长城出

邸志永　席晓靖　赵顺利

起春秋，历秦汉，及辽金，至元明，上下两千年。数不清将帅吏卒，黎庶百工，费尽移山心力，修筑此伟大工程。坚强毅力，聪明智慧，血汗辛勤，为中华留下巍峨丰碑。

跨峻岭，穿荒原，横瀚海，经绝壁，纵横十万里。望不断长龙烽堞，雄关隘口，犹如玉带明珠，点缀成江山锦绣。起伏奔腾，飞舞盘旋，太空遥见，给世界增添壮丽奇观。

每每想起长城，中国文物研究所原所长罗哲文的《长城赞》，就会不自觉出现在脑海里，让人生出无穷自豪之情。初冬的涞源，碧空如洗，正是观赏长城的好时候。记者来到浮图峪长城烟煤洞段，零距离感受承载400多年历史的明长城。

“烟煤洞这段长城，楼台排列十分密集，并且大多保存较好。登高远眺，这里的长城蜿蜒远去，云雾缭绕的时候，如同一条苍龙隐现。”研究长城多年，涞源白石山景区管委会主任刘春阳告诉记者，“涞源县的明长城全长116.5公里，大都依山就势而筑，一般不设敌楼，只设战台和烽火台，险要之处以山险为墙，

烟煤洞长城

平坦之处则敌楼、战台分布密集，符合作战需要。”

之所以修建长城，跟涞源地处的飞狐古道大有关联。在华北平原和西北高原之间，纵卧着绵延千里的太行山，有着“天下之脊”美誉。在古代，穿越太行山、往来晋冀豫三省有八条咽喉要道，被称为“太行八陉”（《尔雅疏》解释：山形连绵中忽断者名“陉”）。八陉中从南向北第六陉，就是涞源、蔚县之间长达70公里的飞狐陉，也被称为“飞狐古道”。在唐朝，飞狐陉便是一条运输路线。到了宋辽“澶渊之盟”后，涞源更是开放的榷场之一。

“在古代，飞狐陉东连紫荆关，西接倒马关，地处咽喉要道，关乎王朝安危，从来都是兵家必争之地。”刘春阳表示，“宋辽对峙时，萧太后数次率大军经飞狐陉侵伐中原。蒙古人发动灭金之战，也从飞狐陉迂回突破，随后占据紫荆关攻陷中都（今北京）。”

明朝作为中国历史上经历战争最多的朝代，276年间共发生578次战争，长城军事体系对明朝的战略意义最为明显。

刘春阳称，明朝初期军事力量强大，明太祖朱元璋先后8次派大将率重兵征伐元朝残余势力。燕王朱棣当了皇帝以后，先后5次亲率大军北征。明朝初期虽然也修建长城，但规模并不大。明太祖朱元璋认为，每十里甚至数十里设置一座烽火台（备战及传讯功能，内配置火器，一台配5—10名守卫），便足以抵挡蒙古军队。

然而，1449年7月，明英宗率25万大军（号称50万）北征瓦剌部（指漠西蒙古），大军在土木堡惨败，明英宗被俘，史称“土木堡之变”。10月，瓦剌军攻克涞源，绕道易县直逼北京，差点让明朝迁都。如果不是于谦的“北京保卫战”获得胜利，明朝国运实难预料。

“土木堡之变”后，瓦剌、鞑靼等蒙古部落不断兴兵侵犯掳掠，明朝的边防政策也由积极进攻转向被动防御，长城的“拱卫”概念明显加深。

历史记载，边境线长达500多公里的宣府镇（今宣化及周边地区），明初时不过200余座烽火台，到了明世宗（1507—1567）嘉靖中期，宣府镇烽火台达到了1800座。与此同时，为了建立拱卫北京的纵深防御体系，保证飞狐陉的安全，明朝逐步在涞源等地修筑了内长城。嘉靖三十年（1551），为保护皇陵和加强京城防务，明朝专门设置了真保镇。

在此期间，受时断时续的战争影响，涞源的长城也在不断完善，其中，大规模修建主要集中于明神宗万历元年至十三年（1573—1585）。如浮图峪长城始建于明代宗景泰二年（1451），城关设守备一名；城关被大水冲毁后，在万历四年（1576）得到重修，驻守武将级别直接提到了参将。彼时，在烽火台的基础上，涞源修起众多边墙、马面、敌楼，将烽火台连在一起，加强了防御能力。

聊到浓处，不经意间太阳已西沉。回望长城，斑驳的城墙和敌楼被夕阳染上一抹金色，仿佛一道蜿蜒曲折的历史长河。

在这条长河中，地处要地的涞源见证了太多权力的游戏，聆听了太多冰与火之歌。

在这条长河中，屹立不倒的长城凝望着南来北往的骡帮，背负着两种文明的需求和梦想，游走在崎岖的飞狐古道上。

在这条长河中，曾经的烽火连天已经远去，长城脚下的革命老区的精准脱贫攻坚战正如火如荼，让27万涞源人绽放笑颜。

烟煤洞长城

The Great Wall on the Feihu Ancient Road —A Witness of Beacon-Fire in History

Di Zhiyong Xi Xiaojing Zhao Shunli

The Great Wall was constructed in more than two thousand years, from the Spring and Autumn Period to Qin and Han dynasties, Liao and Jin dynasties, and finally to Yuan and Ming dynasties. Countless generals, soldiers and workers made painstaking efforts to complete this great project. It is a crystallization of perseverance, wisdom and hard work, and a lofty monument of the Chinese nation.

The Great Wall extends fifty thousand kilometers, traversing mountains, wilderness, seas and precipices. The endless beacon towers, battlements, passes and sally ports look like pearls on a jade belt, which make the landscape more splendid. The Wall fluctuates, gallops, flutters and hovers. It is a rare wonder for the world.

Whenever thinking of the Great Wall, *Ode to the Great Wall* written by Luo Zhewen, the former director of the Cultural Relics Institute, will unconsciously appear in my mind, and arouse a sense of great pride. Under the cloudless blue sky in Laiyuan in the early winter, it is a good time to visit the Great Wall. I came to the bituminous coal cavern section of Fuyutu Great Wall, to take a closer look at the Ming Great Wall, which has a history of more than 400 years.

"This section of the Great Wall in bituminous coal caverns is densely packed with buildings, most of which are well preserved. Gazing into the distance from afar, the Great Wall here winds far away, and when the clouds are lingering, it is like a hidden green dragon. " Having studied the Great Wall for many years, Liu Chunyang, director of Management Committee of Baishi Mountain Scenic Area in Laiyuan County, told the journalist that the Ming Great Wall is 116.5 kilometers in length, whereas most of the ramparts were built in accordance with the mountain terrain. Generally, no watchtowers are built here, only battle platforms and beacon towers. Due to the fact that dangerous places are surrounded by mountains, battle platforms and beacon towers are densely distributed on the flat places, which meets the needs of combat.

The fact that great walls were built was highly connected to Laiyuan's proximity to the Feihu Ancient Road. Between the Northern China Plain and the Northwest Plateau lies the Taihang Mountain stretching over more than a thousand li(one li refers to about one third of an English mile and now has a standard length of a half kilometer), which is also hailed as the "Ridge of the World". In ancient times, there were eight arterial roads running through the Taihang Mountain to connect Shanxi, Hebei and Henan provinces, which were collectively referred to as the "Eight Roads of Taihang"(as stated in the *Erya Annotations*, a "Xing"(road)refers to a path that lies along winding mountains but abruptly ends). Counting from the south to north, the sixth road is the Feihu Road stretching as long as 70 kilometers from Laiyuan to Wei County, which is also called the "Ancient Road of Feihu". It served as a transportation route in the Tang dynasty. After the Treaty of Chanyuan between Song and Liao was reached, Laiyuan's position as an open trade venue was strengthened.

"In ancient times, the Feihu Road connected to Zijingguan in the east and Daomaguan in the west. Covering a place of great strategic importance, the route was of vital importance for the survival of a dynasty and has thus been a place contested by strategic commanders". Liu Chunyang argued that during the confrontation between Song and Liao, Empress Dowager Xiao led armies to invade the Central Plain via the Feihu Road for multiple times. The Mongols' deadly campaigns against Jin was also implemented through outflanking tactics across the Feihu Road, enabling them to occupy Zijingguan and then conquer Zhongdu(today's Beijing).

The Ming Dynasty witnessed the most wars in Chinese History, with 578 wars in 176 years. The Great Wall fortification had the most strategic significance to the Ming Dynasty.

According to Liu Chunyang, the early Ming dynasty had a strong military power. Zhu Yuanzhang, the first emperor of the Ming dynasty, sent eight generals with strong armies to conquer the remaining forces of the Yuan dynasty. After Zhu Di became the emperor, he led the army to the north five times successively. Although the government built the Great Wall in the early Ming dynasty, it was large in scale. Zhu Yuanzhang believed that the fortification would be strong enough to resist the Mongol army by setting up a beacon tower every ten or even dozens of miles(with the function of preparing for war and transmitting information, equipped with firearms and 5 to 10 guards).

However, in July 1449, Emperor Yingzong of the Ming Dynasty led 250,000 troops(known as 500,000)to march north and attacked the tribe of Wala(referring to Moxi Mongolia), the Ming army suffered a disastrous defeat at Tumu Fortress, and Yingzong was captured, which was known as "Tumu Fortress Crisis" in history. In October 1449, the Wala army conquered Laiyuan and reached Beijing by a detour through Yixian County, almost forcing the Ming Dynasty to move the capital. If it were not for Yu Qian's victory in the "Beijing Defense War ", the destiny of the Ming dynasty would be unpredictable.

After the "Tumu Fortress Crisis", Mongol tribes such as Wala and Manchus invaded and plundered continuously, and the frontier defense policy of the Ming dynasty changed from active attack to passive defense accordingly. As a result, the "defensive function" of the Great Wall was greatly strengthened.

Historical records shows that in Xuanfu Town (now Xuanhua and its surrounding area), which was over 500 kilometers along the border, there were no more than 200 beacon towers in the early Ming dynasty. By the mid-Jiajing period of Ming Emperor Shizong(1507-1567), there were 1,800 beacon towers in Xuanfu Town. Meanwhile, in order to establish an in-depth fortification for protecting Beijing and ensuring the safety of the Feihu Road, the Ming government gradually built the Inner Great Wall at Laiyuan and other places. In the 30th year of the Emperor Jiajing's reign(1551), in order to protect the imperial mausoleum and strengthen the defense of the capital, Zhenbao Town was set up, with the general troops stationed in Baoding and the jurisdiction over the Great Wall in Laiyuan and other places, which covers a total length of 390 kilometers.

During this period, the Great Wall of Laiyuan was constantly consolidated under the intermittent threats of war. A large scale renovation took place between the first year to the thirteenth year of Emperor Shenzong of the Ming Dynasty(1573-1585). For example, the Futuyu Great Wall was originally built in the second year of Emperor Daizong or Jingtai of the Ming Dynasty(1451), where a garrison was established at the pass; after being destroyed in a flood, the pass was reconstructed in the fourth year of Emperor Wanli(1576) and the stationed officer was also promoted to the rank of staff general(Canjiang). At that time, a large multitude of flank walls, buttresses and watchtowers were built to connect the beacon towers and strengthen the capability of defense.

We were indulged in our talk. Inadvertently, the sun already set in the west. Looking back at the Great Wall, mottled walls and watchtowers were stained with golden color by the setting sun. It was like a winding river of history.

In this long river, Laiyuan as a strategic spot witnessed too many games of thrones and listened to too many songs of ice and fire.

In this long river, the standing Great Wall gazed at mule gangs to and fro, which trekked on the rugged Feihu Ancient Road, carrying the needs and dreams of two civilizations.

In this long river, flames of battle have gone away, and in the old revolutionary area at the foot of the Great Wall, targeted poverty alleviation is in full swing, which makes 270,000 Laiyuan people give a smile.

涞源长城掠影

张保林

在涞源境内，依山而坐，绵延起伏的明朝长城似一条巨龙彰显着她的神韵，诉说着时光的记忆……

基石(浮图峪)

印迹(孟良城)

涞源长城为内边长城，修建于万历元年至十一年（1573—1583）。长城从涞源县城东北的苦壮石入境，自西南狼牙口出境，在涞源境内的峰峦峡谷间上下腾越，蜿蜒穿行，总长度达116公里。

2006年，河北省文物局组织普查队对涞源长城进行了严格普查。经测查，全线共有敌楼299座、战台42座、烽火台33座。

今天，无论从哪个方向进入涞源，都能够看见长城的雄姿。她像一位耄耋老人，虽然苍老，但仍矍铄。可以想见，饱经风霜的她见证了王朝的兴亡与更替，在涞源大地上留下了浓重的印迹。清朝屈大均对涞源长城有过这样的描述：“长城带天末，古戍接云中。马踏三秋雪，鹰吟万里风。”

The Memory of Time: The Great Wall in Laiyuan

Zhang Baolin

The Great Wall of the Ming Dynasty in Laiyuan, nestling against the top of the mountain, stretches like a giant dragon, showing its romantic charm and telling the memory of time.

As the Inner Great Wall, the Great Wall in Laiyuan was built from the first year to the eleventh year of Wanli in the Ming Dynasty(1573-1583). The Great Wall enters Laiyuan from Kuzhuangshi in the northeast, and exits from Langyakou in the southwest. It winds through mountain peaks and valleys in Laiyuan County, with a total length of 116 kilometers.

In 2006, the Cultural Relics Bureau of Hebei Province organized a team to carry out a stringent investigation about the Great Wall in Laiyuan. The investigation shows that there are 299 watchtowers, 42 battle platforms, and 33 beacon towers.

Today, no matter from which direction you enter Laiyuan, you can see the majestic appearance of the Great Wall. It looks like an octogenarian, aged as it is, but still hale and hearty. It can be visualized that the Great Wall has witnessed the rise and fall of the dynasties and left lasting imprint on the land of Laiyuan. Qu Dajun of the Qing Dynasty once described the Laiyuan Great Wall, "The Great Wall engulfs the top sky, its old rampart touches the clouds. Horses tramp through the snowfield in late Autumn, and hawks screech with wind roaring from a distance."

长城远眺

崇山峻岭苍龙跃　戍边为民保平安

邸志永　刘寒凝　赵顺利　孟海英

12月4日，保定西北，雪后涞源，崇山峻岭间多了一分冷冽。

站在山脊上的浮图峪长城敌楼，抚摸着斑驳残缺的青砖，看着蜿蜒远去的边墙，听着呼啸而过的北风，投身塞上的感觉油然而生。

对此，深有体会的涞源文物保管所所长安志敏说，2002年9月开始长城普查，他们一行4人用时近一年，才将涞源境内长城的“家底”摸清楚。“那时候装备不好，得用百米测绳一步步丈量，用罗盘定好长城的走向。到了12月份测量浮图峪长城的时候，那叫一个冷啊！为了抗寒，每次吃饭都揣一小瓶酒，冷了就喝一小口……”安志敏说，“正是一步步测量、研究，让我深切认识到长城的伟大。”

按照安志敏的说法，南连倒马关、东接紫荆关的涞源明长城，从涞水县金水口城堡入境，至涞源南马庄狼牙口的香炉石村出境，入山西灵丘县上寨。“涞源境内的长城总长122.5公里，其中明长城全长116.5公里，城墙83.5公里，山险33.8公里，敌楼有264座。”安志敏说。涞源长城的楼台修建较早，城墙修筑较晚，在万历元年至

雪色浪漫涞源长城

四年（1573—1576），才用边墙将两者逐渐连为一体。

“根据我们发现的明朝石刻，涞源境内长城大致包括乌龙沟、浮图峪、宁静安、白石口、插箭岭、狼牙口等段落。其中乌龙沟段保存最为完好，白石口段敌楼被破坏得最为厉害。”安志敏说。按照史料记载，涞源境内长城的用料来自外地，不过普查后发现，长城沿途存在不少砖窑，还能发掘出明朝长城砖。由此可见，涞源境内长城多为就地取材。

“很多人觉得，长城不就是一道墙，连着烽火台，能起到多大的作用？”安志敏笑着说，“可不是那么简单！”按照他们的普查和发掘，长城是一道由城墙、敌楼、关城（城堡）、关隘、

插箭岭长城独山城城堡
石刻上还有“万历三年”
字样

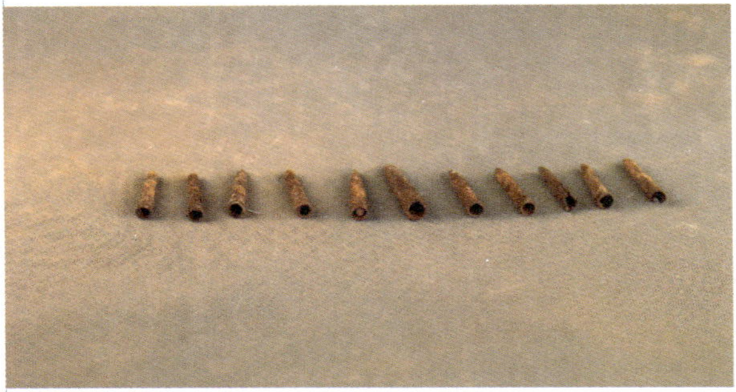

箭帽

涞源长城普查时
发现的箭头

长城防御近战
武器三股叉

涞源插字号石刻

长城远距离攻击的终极武器——红衣大炮

红衣大炮里的铁丸

涞源长城已成摄影爱好者的天堂

荆山口长城

战台、烽火台、马面综合而成的立体军事防御工事。涞源境内的长城，主要是为保护紫荆关而建立的。

以保存最为完好的乌龙沟长城为例。在普查中，安志敏发现，山梁上的长城，在墙外20米左右的地方，往往还设置了一道劈山墙。“这道墙一般都是把山石劈开，直上直下高两三米，让敌人很难直接攻打到长城墙下。如果是在地势较为平坦的地方，古人还会在墙体几十米外设置一道挡马墙，让骑兵很难顺利抵达城墙下。”安志敏说，“在个别重要长城关隘处，古人还会在距离墙体500—1000米的地方，设置一道水门，专门用来放哨、瞭望和侦察。”

即使敌人凶猛，在攻打到长城墙下之前，也要接受“红衣大炮”的轰炸。“前前后后，我们发现了多门长短不一的‘红衣大炮’，以及存放火药、铁砂的瓷瓮，还有一些铁弹丸。在400多年前，这已经是最具威慑力的武器了。”安志敏说，“即使能冲过火器的‘洗礼’，进攻的敌人也得遭遇多轮箭雨。”普查中，他们发现了很多箭杆和金属箭头，有铜质的，也有铁质的。在这样的立体攻击下，敌人会伤亡惨重。最终能攻打到城墙下的敌人还得面临礌石、滚木等自上而下的攻击。“好不容易爬到城头，敌人会发现迎面而来的是红缨枪和三股叉的穿刺。”安志敏说。普查中，他们发现了一些金属质红缨枪和三股叉，虽经历了400多年风雨，但其看上去仍锋利无比。

“烽火台、敌楼、关隘、边墙，以及各种防御装备和驻守士兵，共同构成了长城军事体系。”安志敏说，“在没有长城军事体系的明朝初期，游牧民族劫掠内地的记载非常多。随着长城的逐步完善，虽然仍有游牧民族‘毁墙而入’的记载，但情况已大为改观。”

“日拱一卒无有尽，功不唐捐终入海。”时光回溯到400多年前的明嘉靖年间，对于耗费巨资和时间修建长城，当时的士大夫们同样有着清醒而深刻的认知。

明朝学者陈全之创作的《蓬窗日录》中，多角度对修建长城做了肯定性论述。文章称，随着长城军事体系的修建，胡虏入侵大为减少，百姓更愿意在边塞居住，部队的士气提升了，境内的环境更加安全了，粮食的价格下降了，经商环境也大为改善。

时光荏苒，历史硝烟散去，而今留下的是盛世的宁静与祥和。在实现中华民族伟大复兴的宏伟目标下，作为中华民族精神象征的长城不再是保护人民的防御工事，而是一笔亟须保护和发掘的历史财富。在这笔堪称无价的财富中，我们庆幸涞源境内的长城，经历400多年风雨后，依旧保存较为完好，等来属于它的觉醒。

雪色浪漫涞源长城

The Futuyu Great Wall — A Green Dragon Defending the Border on Steep Mountains

Di Zhiyong Liu Hanning Zhao Shunli Meng Haiying

On December 4, in Laiyuan, northwest Baoding, it became colder in snow-covered mountains.

Standing in a watchtower of the Futuyu Great Wall on a mountain ridge, touching the mottled, incomplete black bricks, looking at the flank walls winding forward, and listening to the whistling north wind, it is a typical feeling of being on a fort.

An Zhimin, Director of Cultural Relics Protection Institute of Yixian County, had much to say about this. In September 2002, a general investigation of the Great Wall was started. He and the other three men spent nearly one year finding out the situation of the Great Wall in Laiyuan. "At that time, our equipment was underdeveloped. We measured step by step with a 100m rope, and determined the direction of the Great Wall with a compass. When we measured the Futuyu Great Wall in December, how cold it was! In order to resist the cold, I took a small bottle of wine and sipped it whenever I could not bear the cold..." said An Zhimin. It was the measurement and investigation step by step that made him deeply realize the greatness of the Great Wall.

According to An Zhimin, the Ming Great Wall in Laiyuan is connected to Daomaguan in the south and Zijingguan in the east. It extends from Jinshuikou Fort in Laishui County to Xianglushi Village at Langyakou of Nanmazhuang Village, and enters Lingqiu County in Shanxi Province." The total length of the Great Wall in Laiyuan is 122.5 kilometers, of which the Ming Great Wall is 116.5 kilometers long. The total length of the rampart is 83.5 kilometers long, and narrow mountain pass is 33.8 kilometers long. There are 264 watchtowers." An Zhimin said. The watchtowers of Laiyuan Great Wall were constructed earlier, while the ramparts were built later. It was from the first year to the fourth year of Wanli period(1573-1576)that they were gradually connected together through flank walls.

An Zhimin said, "According to the stone carvings of the Ming Dynasty, the Great Wall in Laiyuan roughly includes the sections in Wulonggou, Futuyu, Ningjing'an, Baishikou, Chajianling and Langyakou. Among them, the Wulonggou section is the most well-preserved, and the watchtowers in Baishikou is most severely damaged." According to historical records, the building materials of the Great Wall in Laiyuan came from other places. After the investigation, it was found that there were many brick kilns along the Great Wall, and bricks of Ming Dynasty could also be excavated. It can be seen that the Great Wall in Laiyuan was mostly constructed with local building materials.

"Many people think that the Great Wall is just a rampart connected to beacon towers. How much of a difference could it make? " An Zhimin said with a smile, "It's not that simple!" According to the results of their investigation and excavation, the Great Wall is a three-dimensional military fortification composed of ramparts, watchtowers, forts, mountain passes, battle platforms, beacon towers and buttresses. The Great Wall in Laiyuan was mainly built to protect Zijingguan.

Take the best preserved Wulonggou Great Wall as an example. In the general investigation, An Zhimin found that a gable was usually set up about 20 meters outside the Great Wall on the mountain ridge. To build the gable, rocks were split in most places. The wall generally stands two or three meters tall, so that it is difficult for the enemy to reach the foot of the Great Wall. In flat areas, the ancients set up a horse-fending wall tens of meters away from the rampart to prevent cavalry from approaching the wall. An Zhimin said, "In several vital Great Wall passes, the ancient people would build a water gate 500 to 1,000 meters away from the rampart, which was specially used for sentry, lookout and reconnaissance."

Enemies were bombed by "Hongyi Cannons" before they reached the foot of the Great Wall. "We successively discovered a number of 'Hongyi Cannons' of different lengths, as well as earthen jars for storing gunpowder and iron sand, and iron projectiles. More than 400 years ago, it was the most deterrent weapon," said An Zhimin. "Those who luckily survived firearms had to suffer rain of arrows." During the surveys, they found many arrow shafts and metal arrows, made of either copper or iron. Under such a three-dimensional attack, enemies would suffer heavy casualties. Enemies who could finally make it to the ramparts had to suffer top-down attacks of boulders and rolling logs. "after climbing to the top of the rampart, they would find themselves confronted with the red-tasselled spears and the three-pronged forks." An Zhimin said. During the investigation, they found some red-tasselled spears and three-pronged forks, which still look sharp despite more than 400 years of wind and rain.

"Beacon towers, watchtowers, mountain passes, flank walls, together with various defensive equipments and garrisons together constitute the Great Wall military system." An Zhimin said, "In the early Ming Dynasty, when the Great Wall fortification had not yet been established, there were numerous records of nomads plundering inland. With the gradual improvement of the Great Wall, there were still records of nomads 'breaking into the ramparts', but the situation had changed greatly."

One step a day leads to a destination away. Back to more than 400 years ago, the scholar-bureaucrats of the Jiajing Period of the Ming Dynasty had clear and profound awareness of huge sums of money and time spent on the construction of the Great Wall.

Chen Quanzhi, a scholar of the Ming Dynasty, wrote a book entitled *A Window Diary* on social economics, in which he made positive comments on the construction of the Great Wall from various perspectives. According to the article, with the development of the Great Wall fortification, the number of intrusions of the Hu people was greatly reduced, people were more willing to live in the frontier area, the morale of the troops was promoted, the domestic environment was safer, food prices declined, and the business environment was greatly improved.

Time flies. After the smoke of gunpowder dissipated, what remains is peace and serenity today. Under the grand goal of realizing the great rejuvenation of the Chinese nation, the Great Wall, as a symbol of the spirit of Chinese nation, is no longer a fortification to protect the people, but a historical treasure that needs to be protected and excavated urgently. Fortunately, as a invaluable treasure, the Great Wall in Laiyuan is still well-preserved after over 400 years of wind and rain, and is waiting for its awakening.

南楼台长城

关山脚下话姓氏

张洁　吴战平

冬日的涞源县下北头乡插箭岭村，阳光渐强，薄雾消散，村委会院内一整面铜墙上浮雕的78个姓氏愈发清晰可辨，与远处伏于山脊的“苍龙”遥相呼应，仿若诉说着数百年前的烽烟历史。

“邨者，人群居、生息之所也，然曰屯兵而形成村落者，惟插箭岭邨而已。”姓氏是祖辈留下的根基，有些地方全村都是同一姓氏，甚至有的村名都以姓氏命名，而插箭岭村210户人家姓氏如此之多，个中缘由透过铜墙上开篇的话可窥一二。

村党支部书记火红旺介绍：“插箭岭段长城始建于明朝嘉靖年间，属于‘内三关’之一的倒马关。村里姓氏多，就是因为这里戍边将士多，要么举家迁来，要么在这里成家落户，现在村里还有当年戍边人的后代。”

火红旺言之凿凿，也确有据可寻。据明朝《四镇三关志》所载，真保镇军旅客兵一万九千八百四十三名万历元年侍郎汪道昆经略定为令额。插箭岭属真保镇所辖范围，“客兵”意为外地调来的军队，由此可知明朝时的确有不少外来的士兵。这也符合明朝兵制特点，本籍军户一般不在本地卫所从军，军士皆别立户籍，叫军户，军户世袭，军人家属也要和军人一道到卫戍地居住。

由此再看插箭岭的姓氏，出现诸如南方常见的吴姓、山东常见的孟姓等，也就不足为奇了。

插箭岭村并不是个例，保定境内长城脚下的村庄普遍姓氏丰富。“内三关”之一的紫荆关位于易县境内，紫荆关长城脚下村庄姓氏聚集更加明显。紫荆关镇25个村姓氏多达140余个。

《易县志》在《族源》一节有明确记载：“明代回族人迁入定居较多，分别住于西亢各庄、大巨、塘湖、神石庄等村。西亢各村董姓回民为明代镇守紫荆关的武职官员携眷落户于该村。”这更加印证了明朝兵制对姓氏聚集的影响。

除此之外，长城对于附近村落而言本身就有地缘优势，这也是姓氏聚集不容忽略的一点。

正如《明史·方逢时传》所载：“九边生齿日繁，守备日固，田野日辟，商贾日通，边民始知有生之乐。”明朝大规模修建长城，屯田实边，互市贸易随之增多，长城脚下的村落自然成了四面八方的商贩汇聚之地，吸引着不同民族和地域的人们在此落地生根。

历经数百年的风雨和朝代更迭，昔日的明守军后裔已完全融入当地人的生活。紫荆关镇镇长张建军说：“我们镇的人口在抗日战争时期由于日军的占领曾出现过锐减，之后一直相对稳定。随着农村政策越来越好，农村人口更加稳定，除个别姓氏的自然消亡外，近些年各村的姓氏几乎没变化。”

慎终追远的姓氏文化，作为根祖文化的一部分，在古城保定与长城文化、商贸文化相伴相生，是特殊的历史印记。我国姓氏

紫荆关长城脚下村庄

文化源远流长，姓氏文化是民族文化的一个缩影，透过“百家姓”，能够洞悉一个地域的历史文化进程。在谈及姓氏文化的发掘和保护时，对长城文化有着多年调查研究的河北大学博物馆副馆长李文龙说：“来自不同地域的不同姓氏、家族聚集在一起，必然带来不同的文化、习俗等，对地域多元文化的发展有促进作用。发掘姓氏文化要重视发动民间力量寻祖，激发群众对自己祖先留下来的文化遗产的热爱，从而在长城文化遗产保护中发挥积极作用。”

（历史文化顾问：

直隶总督署博物馆吴蔚）

Surname Culture at the Foot of Guan Mountain

Zhang Jie　Wu Zhanping

It was a winter day in Chajianling Village of Xiabeitou Town, Laiyuan County. The sunlight was getting stronger, and the mist was dissipating. The 78 embossed surnames on a whole copper wall in the courtyard of the Village Committee looked clearer and more discernible at this moment. It echoed with the "Black Dragon" lying on the distant ridge. They seemed to be telling the stories of beacon-fire hundreds of years ago.

"Village is a place for villagers to stay and make a living. Chajianling Village is a only place that was formed by soldiers of garrisons who settled down here." Surnames are the roots of ancestors in villages. In some places all the people in a village has the same surname, and even some villages are named after surnames. The reason why there are so many surnames among the 210 families in Chajianling Village can be seen through the opening remarks embossed on the bronze wall.

Huo Hongwang, Secretary of the Village Party Branch, said, "The section of the Great Wall in chajianling was built in the Emperor Jiajing period of the Ming Dynasty. It belongs to Daomaguan, one of the 'Three Inner Passes'. The large number of surnames in the village is due to the large number of garrison soldiers, who either moved their families here or settled down here. There are still descendants of those soldiers in the village."

Indeed, evidence can be found despite the overconfidence in Huo Hongwang's words. According to *Historical Records of Four Towns and Three Passes*, Zhenbao Town(the general commander was stationed in Baoding, governing 390 kilometers of the Great Wall in Laiyuan and other areas) was once guarded by 19,843 military personnel and alien soldiers. In the first year of Emperor Wanli's rein, Wang Daokun, the assistant minister, submitted a plan to designate the quota of military persons that stationed here. Chajianling fell into the governing territory of Zhenbao Town. "Alien soldiers" refer to troops recruited from other areas. As can be seen, there were indeed a large number of alien soldiers in the Ming dynasty. Such a system was also consistent with the characteristics of the conscription system at the time. Native military households generally did not serve locally. Separate household registrations were created for families with military members, which were called military households. The title could be passed down to future generations. Civilian members of military households could reside at the garrison along with military members.

It is not surprising that the surnames of families in Chajianling Village, such as the surname of Wu in south China and Meng in Shandong, were originated.

Chajianling Village is not an exception. A great variety of surnames can be found in the villages at the foot of the Great Wall in Baoding. Zijingguan, one of the "Three Inner Passes", is located in Yixian County, and the cluster of surnames in villages at the foot of the Zijingguan Great Wall is more obvious. There are more than 140 surnames in the 25 villages of Zijingguan Town.

Clear records can be found in the section of *Clan Origin of Yixian County Chronicles*, "During the Ming Dynasty, a great number of Hui people settled down in Yixian County, living in Xikangge, Daju, Tanghu, Shenshizhuang and other villages. In Xikangge village, the Hui people with the surname of Dong were proved to be the military officials who were stationed at Zijingguan in the Ming Dynasty and settled down in the village with their families." It further confirms the influence of the Ming Dynasty military system on the cluster of surnames.

In addition, the Great Wall itself has geographical advantages for the nearby villages, which is also a factor that contributes to the surname aggregation.

As recorded by *The History of Ming: Biography of Fang Fengshi,* "people living around the borders did not feel any pleasure in life until the population at the northern borders got increasingly larger, the garrisons got increasingly strengthened, more waste land was cultivated, trade became increasingly active." The government of the Ming Dynasty put in great efforts to build the Great Wall and dispatch military households to cultivate border land, and then the volume of border trade significantly increased. Villages at the foot of the Great Wall naturally became gathering places for merchants from various places, attracting people from different ethnic origins and locations to settle down here.

After hundreds of years of wind and rain and the change of dynasties, the descendants of the Ming Dynasty Garrisons have fully integrated into local life. Zhang Jianjun, mayor of Zijingguan Town, said, "The population of our town dropped sharply due to the Japanese occupation during the Anti-Japanese War, and has remained relatively stable ever since. With better rural policies and a more stable rural population, surnames in the village have barely changed in recent years, with the exception of the natural extinction of individual surnames."

As a part of the ancestral culture, surname culture is associated with the Great Wall culture and business culture in the ancient city of Baoding, which is a special historical mark. Surname culture, which has a long history in China, is an epitome of national culture. Through "hundred surnames", we can have a clear understanding of the historical and cultural development of a region. When talking about the exploration and protection of surname culture, Li Wenlong, deputy director of Hebei University Museum, who has studied the Great Wall culture for many years, said, "The gathering of surnames and families from different regions inevitably brings the culture and customs of the local places, which promotes the development of diversified

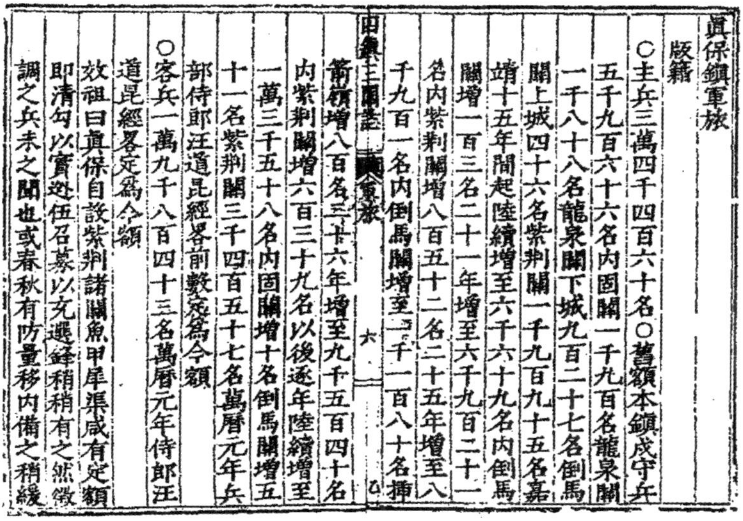

真保鎮軍旅

版籍

○主兵三萬四千四百六十名○舊額本鎮戍守兵五千九百六十六名内固關一千九百名龍泉關一千八十八名龍泉關下城九百二十七名倒馬關上城四十六名紫荆關一千九百九十五名嘉靖十五年間起陸續增至六千六十九名内倒馬關增一百三名二十一年增至六千九百二十一名内紫荆關增八百五十二名二十五年增至八千九百一名内倒馬關增至二千一百八十名挿箭嶺增八百名三十六年增至九千五百四十名内紫荆關增六百三十九名以後遂年陸續增至一萬三千五十八名内固關增十名倒馬關增五十一名紫荆關三千四百五十七名萬曆元年兵部侍郎汪道昆經畧前數定爲今額

○客兵一萬九千八百四十三名萬曆元年侍郎汪道昆經畧定爲今額

效祖曰真保自設紫荆諸關魚甲犀渠咸有定額即清勾以實逃伍召募以充選鋒稍稍有之然徵調之兵未之聞也或春秋有防量移内備之稍緩

四鎮三關志 軍旅 六

史10—87

《四镇三关志》
(李文龙提供)

regional cultures. To explore surname culture, we should mobilize the folk forces to trace the origin of ancestors and arouse people's affection for the cultural heritage left by ancestors, so as to play a positive role in the protection of the Great Wall as a cultural heritage."

(The consultant on history and culture: Wu Wei, staff member of Zhili Governor's Office Museum)

紫荆关城百战多 将士英名留青史

赵丰民 杨虎 吴战平 于万正

古老的紫荆关，对于年轻的易县文物保管所副所长贾国琳来说，太熟悉了。她每年来往紫荆关多次，进行调查和研究，积累了丰富的史料。说起紫荆关的历史，尤其在紫荆关发生的战事，她如数家珍。

隆冬时节，我们驱车到紫荆关采访。贾国琳热情地为我们讲解，目前紫荆关的关墙总长18 160.5米，共有城门9座、水门4座、战台19座。雄关壮丽，地势险要，自古就是人们反复争夺的军事要地，素有“畿南第一雄关”之称。

今日之紫荆关，雄险不减，山峦叠翠，更显风骨。

顺着贾国琳手指的方向望去，紫荆关城门巍峨矗立，城门上方，“河山带砺”四字在冬日阳光的照耀下熠熠生辉。

贾国琳介绍，紫荆关东汉时称“五阮关”，北魏时称“子庄关”，宋朝称为“金坡关”，明朝以后称为“紫荆关”。初为土石夯筑，后历经各朝代扩建、修葺，到明洪武初年，则改用石条作基础，以砖砌面封顶，并用石灰碎石灌注。明成祖迁都北平（今北京）后，大兴土木，修城建关。在正统、景泰、弘治、嘉

紫荆关长城墙体

靖、万历、崇祯年间，统治者都曾改筑、扩建关城，增设城堡、隘口，开凿盘山道等，使紫荆关形成了一个较完备的防御体系。

紫荆关战略位置重要，历来为兵家必争之地。史料记载，明臣于谦说："险有轻重，则守有缓急，居庸、紫荆并为畿辅咽喉，论者尝先居庸，而后紫荆，不知寇窥居庸其得入者十之三，寇窥紫荆其得入者十之七。"明末清初时期的思想家顾炎武描述："居庸则吾之背也，紫荆则吾之喉也，猝有急则扼吾之喉而附吾之背。"这些都可凸显出紫荆关战略地位的重要性。

登上城墙看紫荆关，关城四周群峦环抱，沟壑纵横，地势险峻。远处望去，拒马河从西边山谷缓缓而来，紫荆关依偎在拒马河边，起伏在丘陵之间，将山谷牢牢锁定。

紫荆关关城由5个大小不等的城圈组成，呈梅花状。它曾是军事防御指挥机关所在地。据《西关志》记载，明朝景泰二年（1451），调保定右卫中千户所官军守御本关，景泰三年

（1452），添设真定、神武二位官军，春秋两班轮流操守。清初紫荆关仍设参将驻守。“虽然紫荆关城门楼大都已经荒废，但古代这里有完整的军事防御体系，少时几百人，最多时候驻军3000余人。”贾国琳说，“历史上，许多著名战事都与紫荆关有密切联系，据不完全统计，在紫荆关发生的战事有百余次。”

紫荆关绵长的城墙雄姿犹在，望着紫荆关长城上厚重的墙体和一个个垛口，我们仿佛听到了战场上那阵阵喊杀声、战马的嘶鸣声，一段段逝去的历史浮现在眼前。

史料记载，宋嘉定六年（1213）秋，成吉思汗率领蒙古大军与金兵大战，金败，蒙古大军追至北口，攻打居庸关，因金兵严密镇守无法进入。于是蒙古大军又前往涿鹿至紫荆关，在紫荆关南百二十里的五回岭击败金兵，进而轻取涿州、易州两地，进入内地。又到南口由内而外攻打居庸关，将居庸关攻破。

“这场战役是紫荆关历史上发生的百余次战役中最著名的一次。此后，紫荆关又多次成为蒙古军征战内地的重要出入关口。”贾国琳说。

由于紫荆关在军事进攻和防御上的重要位置，自古便于此设关口。明正统年间的“土木堡之变”中，瓦刺军攻陷紫荆关直逼京师。明朝通过“北京保卫战”最终击退瓦刺进攻，进一步认识到紫荆关一线的军事重要性。明朝在修复、扩大宣大（今宣化、大同）一线长城规模的同时，严密增加了居庸关以南，经紫荆关至倒马关一线的长城防守。今日之所谓“内三关”，即由此而来。

说起紫荆关的古战役战将，贾国琳提到了明军右副都御史孙祥和清军总统陕军的山西布政使升允。

明正统十四年（1449），蒙古族瓦剌首领也先兵分四路对长城沿线侵扰。7月于土木堡击溃明军，俘获明英宗朱祁镇。瓦剌部经过短暂休整，于10月1日兵分三路。东路2万骑由古北口攻密云，从侧翼牵制明军。中路5万骑由兴和（今张北）经宣府（今宣化）攻居庸关，做正面佯攻。瓦剌太师也先亲率10万骑为西路，自集宁经大同攻紫荆关，遭明军右副都御史孙祥、都指挥韩清的顽强抗击。十月初九日，兵临关下，也先令太监喜宁向守军传达英宗旨意开城，遭明军拒绝。遂以主力在关城正面与明军对峙，另遣一部由喜宁带路，寻山间小路偷越紫荆岭，绕至关南，拆毁边墙而入。

明军腹背受敌，因寡不敌众，孙祥等明军将士全部战死，关城被攻陷。也先率大军长驱直入，直逼北京城。

到了清朝，关城已成腹地，但是兵额未减，康熙曾两次西巡，驻跸紫荆关，检阅军校，南天门曾立有“天子阅武处”碑。

史料记载，1900年，八国联军发动了侵华战争，8月14日攻占北京。10月，英、德、法、意四国联军直扑山西，进逼直隶、山西边界重关——紫荆关。紫荆关城池高深，嵯峨险峻，左右崖壁陡峭笔直，犹如天然屏障，是北京西南的重要关隘。当总统陕军的山西布政使升允得知联军西犯时，立即率右翼马队进驻紫荆关，并派两营陕军分守紫荆关西南的五回岭、倒马关、走马驿等百里以内各要隘，留一营陕军镇守紫荆关。10月28日，升允照会联军指挥官，试图劝止敌军继续西犯，侵略军不予理睬。10月29日黎明，尖厉刺耳的枪炮声划破长城寂静的上空，配有坚枪利炮的联军突然向紫荆关发起猛烈进攻，升允遂率清军应战，清军将士英勇顽强坚守阵地，与侵略者展开了一场殊死战斗。经过激战，紫荆关失守，清军阵亡

冬日紫荆关长城，拒马河从山脚下静静流过

87位将士。

“紫荆关之战虽然失败了，但是清军将士英勇无畏、誓死抵抗到底的英雄气概狠狠打击了侵略者的嚣张气焰，阻止了侵略军继续西犯。”贾国琳说。

1903年6月，已任山西巡抚的升允为了纪念那些在紫荆关之战中为国捐躯的英烈，下令在紫荆关盘道寺墙上镌刻了一段中国人民英勇抗击八国联军侵略的碑文，碑文中记录了87位捐躯的清军将士姓名。同年，受德国驻华公使的压力，清政府派人撤毁石碑。

“石碑虽然不在了，但中国将士英勇抗击八国联军的精神浩气长存。”贾国琳说，“紫荆关边塞苦寒，多练就侠肝义胆。历史上的紫荆关，每有烽烟起，战旗便在此地红。”

（历史文化顾问：河北大学博物馆副馆长、教授李文龙）

Zijingguan—A Place Known for Frequent Wars and Brave Generals

Zhao Fengmin　Yang Hu　Wu Zhanping　Yu Wanzheng

The ancient Zijingguan is rather familiar to Jia Guolin, the young deputy director of Yixian County Cultural Relics Reservation Center. She traveled to and from Zijingguan many times every year, to conduct investigation and research, and accumulated a wealth of historical materials. Speaking of the history of Zijingguan, especially the wars that took place there, she undoubtedly knows everything.

In the middle of winter, we drove to Zijingguan for an interview. Jia Guolin enthusiastically explained to us that the total length of the ramparts at Zijingguan is 18,160.5 meters, with 9 city gates, 4 water gates, and 19 battle platforms. With magnificent fortresses and precipitous terrain, Zijingguan has been an important military area that was repeatedly contested by strategic commanders since ancient times. It is known as "the No. 1 Impregnable Pass in Ji'nan".

Today's Zijingguan, standing among verdant mountains, still keeps its magnificence and precipitousness and shows its strength of character.

Jia pointed to the gate of Zijingguan. The city gate of Zijingguan stands towering, and above the gate, the four characters "He Shan Dai Li"(meaning one's resolution will not be even the slightest shaken over time) are shining brightly in the winter sunshine. Jia Guolin introduced that Zijingguan was called "Wuruanguan" in the Eastern Han Dynasty, "Zizhuangguan" in the

Northern Wei Dynasty, "Jinpoguan" in the Song Dynasty, and "Zijingguan" after the Ming Dynasty. At first it was built with earth and stone, while after various generations of expansion and renovation, in the early years of Hongwu in the Ming Dynasty, striped stones were used as the foundation, the roof was sealed with bricks, and grouted with lime gravel. After Ming Emperor Chengzu moved the capital to Beiping(Beijing), he made great efforts to rebuild the city. During the years of Zhengtong, Jingtai, Hongzhi, Jiajing, Wanli, and Chongzhen, Zijingguan was rebuilt and expanded. Meanwhile, pass cities, fortresses, sally forts, and winding mountain roads were built, so that a relatively complete fortification was eastablished at Zijingguan.

Given its strategic importance, Zijingguan has long been a place contested by many strategic commanders. Yu Qian, a famous military leader in the Ming Dynasty, said, "Just as there are different degrees of dangers, there are also different levels of urgency in defense. Juyongguan and Zijingguan are both vital fortresses defending the capital city. However, military commentators often put Juyongguan above Zijingguan, without knowing the fact that invaders are able to achieve 3 successes out of 10 attempts at Juyongguan but 7 successes out of 10 attempts at Zijingguan". "If Juyongguan is the back of our deployment, then Zijingguan is the throat. Sudden emergencies would arise if our throat gets choked and our back captured", as described by Gu Yanwu, a thinker during the late Ming and early Qing period. All these statements highlight the strategic importance of Zijingguan.

Viewing Zijingguan from the top of the rampart, one could see that the pass city is surrounded by mountains with deep ravines and sitting on an environment of precipitous topography. Watching from afar, one could see the Juma River gradually stretches from the western valley to partially enclose the Zijingguan which rises and falls along with the hills and firmly locks down the valley.

Zijingguan City is composed of five city rings one in another, which is overall lotus-shaped. It used to be the seat of the military defense command. According to the *Xiguan Chronicles*, in the second year of Jingtai in the Ming Dynasty(1451), some generals and soldiers of Baoding Garrison were assigned to defend this pass. In the 3rd year of Jingtai (1452), two generals, Zhending and Shenwu, were added to defend the pass alternately in spring or autumn. Generals were also assigned to garrison the city in the early Qing Dynasty. "Although the gate tower has been almost abandoned, there was a complete fortification here in ancient times. The garrison numbered hundreds to 3,000," said Jia Guolin. "In history, many famous wars were closely related to Zijingguan. Based on incomplete statistics, the wars that happened at Zijingguan exceeded one hundred."

The majestic appearance of the city wall of Zijingguan remains. Looking at the heavy wall and crenels in series, I feel as if I heard the shouts of soldiers and the neighing of war horses on the battlefield. The fragments of history flooded into my mind.

According to historical records, in the autumn of the sixth year of Jiading in the Song Dynasty(1213), Genghis Khan led the Mongol army to fight against the Jin army. After the Jin army was defeated, the Mongol army chased to the north exit and attacked Juyongguan, but was unable to enter because of the tight guards of the Jin soldiers. So the Mongol army went from Zhuolu to Zijingguan, defeated the Jin army at Wuhuiling where is located 60 kilometers south of Zijingguan, and then captured Zhuozhou and Yizhou easily and entered inland. Afterwards, Genghis Khan went to the south exit to attack Juyongguan from inside and breached it.

"This battle is the most famous one among more than a hundred battles in the history of Zijingguan. Since then, Zijingguan had repeatedly became an important gateway for the Mongol army to enter and exit inland." Jia Guolin said.

Due to the important position of Zijingguan in military offense and defense, it has been convenient to set up the pass since ancient times. The "Tumu Fortress Crisis" occurred during Zhengtong period of the Ming Dynasty, and the Wala Army captured Zijingguan and approached the capital. Although the "Beijing Defense War" finally repelled the attack of the Wala Army, the emperor of the Ming Dynasty further realized the military importance of Zijingguan. In the Ming Dynasty, the Great Wall at Xuanda (now Xuanhua and Datong)were renovated and its scale was expanded.

Meanwhile, the defense of the Great Wall from the south of Juyongguan to Daomaguan via Zijingguan were also strengthened. Today's so-called "Three Inner Passes" came from this.

Speaking of the ancient generals at Zijingguan, Jia Guolin mentioned Sun Xiang, the right deputy officer of the Court of Censors in the Ming army, and Sheng Yun, commissioner of Shanxi and Shaanxi in the Qing army.

In the fourteenth year of Zhengtong in the Ming Dynasty(1449), the Mongol Wala leader divided the troops into four groups to invade along the Great Wall. In July, he defeated the Ming army in Tumu Fortress and captured Zhu Qizhen, Emperor Yingzong of the Ming Dynasty. After a short rest and reorganization, the Wala Army was divided into three groups on October 1st. Twenty thousand cavalries on the East Road attacked Miyun from Gubeikou and pinned down the Ming army from the flank, while fifty thousand cavalries on the middle road attacked Juyongguan from Xinghe(now Zhangbei County)via Xuanfu (now Xuanhua), making a frontal feint. Taishi of Wala also personally led 100,000 cavalries to the west, and attacked Zijingguan from Jining via Datong. He was tenaciously resisted by Sun Xiang, the right deputy officer of the Court of Censors in the Ming army, and the commander Han Qing. On October 9th, when the soldiers came to the border, Ye Xian asked the eunuch Xining to convey Emperor Yingzong's order to open the city, but the Ming army rejected it. So he led the main force to confront the Ming army in the front of Zijingguan city, and dispatched another group of soldiers led by Xining, who managed to sneak across Zijing Ridge via mountain paths, detoured to the south of Zijingguan City, demolished the flank walls and broke into the city.

The Ming army was attacked in front and rear. Because they were outnumbered, Sun Xiang and other soldiers were all killed in the battle, and Zijingguan was captured. Ye Xian led his army straight into Beijing.

By the Qing Dynasty, Zijingguan had became a hinterland, but the number of garrisons had not been reduced. Emperor Kangxi had made an inspection tour to the west twice, stationed at Zijingguan, and reviewed the military academy. A stele inscribed with the "Place where the Emperor Inspected His Army" in Nantianmen.

According to historical records, in 1900, the Eight-Nation Allied Forces launched a war of aggression against China and captured Beijing on August 14. In October, the allied forces of Britain, Germany, France, and Italy attacked Shanxi directly, advancing towards Zijingguan, an important pass located in the border between Zhili and Shanxi. The Zijingguan city wall and moat is high and deep, with precipitous cliffs around like a natural barrier. Therefore, it is an important passage in the southwest of Beijing. When Sheng Yun, commissioner of Shanxi and Shaanxi army, learned that the allied forces were marching to the west, he immediately led the right-wing cavalry to station at Zijingguan, dispatched two battalions of Shaanxi troops to guard Wuhuiling, Daomaguan, Zoumayi and other passes within fifty kilometers in the southwest of Zijingguan, and leaving a battalion of Shaanxi Army to guard Zijingguan. On October 28th, Sheng Yun delivered a note to the commander of the allied forces, trying to persuade the enemy not to continue to invade the west, but the invading army ignored it. At dawn on October 29, the piercing sound of guns broke through the silent sky over the Great Wall. The allied forces with well-equipped armed guns and artillery suddenly launched a fierce attack on Zijingguan. Sheng Yun led the Qing army to fight back, and the Qing soldiers guarded their positions bravely and tenaciously, and launched a desperate battle with the invaders. After fierce battles, Zijingguan was conquered, and 87 officers and Qing soldiers were killed.

"Although Qing soldiers were defeated in the battle of Zijingguan, the heroic spirit of the Qing army, who fought against the invaders bravely and fearlessly, severely hit the arrogant invaders and prevented the invading army from continuing to invade the west." Jia Guolin said.

In June 1903, in order to commemorate those heroes who died for the country in the battle of Zijingguan, Sheng Yun, the commissioner of Shanxi, ordered to engrave an inscription on the wall of the Pandao Temple in Zijingguan, which referred to Chinese people's heroic resistance to the invasion of the Eight-Nation Allied Forces. The inscriptions recorded the names of 87 Qing soldiers who died for the country. In the same year, under the pressure from the German envoy in China, the Qing government sent people to remove and destroy the stele.

"Although the stele is no longer there, the spirit of the Chinese soldiers who fought bravely against the Eight-Nation Allied Forces will never perish." Jia Guolin said, "Zijingguan is a bitter and cold frontier fortress, where most of the soldiers had honed their chivalrous and gallant spirit. In the history of Zijingguan, whenever there was beacon fire, the battle flag would be flying here."

(The consultant on history and culture: Professor Li Wenlong, deputy curator and professor of Hebei University Museum)

饱经风霜仍坚毅　涞源长城展风华

邸志永　刘寒凝　王栋

2019年12月24日下午，河北涞源县乌龙沟乡柱角石村，村边乌龙河波光粼粼，远处山峦间残雪未消。

手拄从农家借来的登山杖，怀揣对“最美野长城”的期待，记者随涞源县文物保管所所长安志敏踏雪寻城，聊起关于涞源长城保护的点点滴滴。

“乌龙沟长城有71座敌楼，只有7座损毁，经历400多年烽火和自然侵蚀，能保存成这样，在全国都比较罕见。”安志敏说。涞源长城并非都如乌龙沟段保存这般完好。“涞源长城所在地段，很多都是交通要道。抗日战争时期，这些占据制高点的长城敌楼，经常是敌我双方争夺的焦点。如插箭岭长城的敌楼，抗战时从4号楼一直拆到了27号楼。浮图峪、宁静安等段长城，也都遭受了战火。”安志敏说，“涞源境内一共269座敌楼，如果都保存完好，申请世界文化遗产都有希望。”

除了自然侵蚀和战火损毁之外，人为损坏也是一大原因。受社会经济条件影响，一些长城附近的居民在盖房子时，往往会拆长城的砖石。“在水堡镇独山城村，很多20世纪二三十年代建造的老房子，地基都是用的长城基石。”安志敏说，“到了20世纪70年代，修建保涞公路，也拆了一部分长城。此后，修建涞源钢厂时，一些长城基石也被拆走做了厂矿地基。”

2002年9月，安志敏和文物保管所工作人员一起做长城普查时，发现保存较好的乌龙沟长城的很多敌楼被羊倌用来做羊圈。彼时的涞源铜矿、铁矿较多，在一些长城脚下开矿建厂，对长城也威胁极大。

亡羊补牢，为时未晚。人们保护长城的意识，也在不断觉醒。

20世纪50年代，涞源境内明长城乌龙沟段成了河北省文物保护单位。1999年，涞源县为乌龙沟长城申报了全国重点文物保护单位，于2001年通过审核。2002年长城普查开始，随着发现的问题越来越多，当地政府对长城的关注力度也不断增强。“2002

修缮后的涞源县乌龙沟长城10号烽火台

涞源县乌龙沟长城

年，我们专门成立了‘长城保护员’队伍，选择了7名责任心强的村民，加强对长城的巡视守护。”涞源县旅游文物局局长靳二楞说，“至今长城保护员已经发展到21名，他们每周汇报一次所负责段长城的保护工作。”

村民的保护意识也在增强。2004年，浮图峪长城被一个选矿厂老板开铲车挖掉了63米城墙，村民举报后，破坏者被判刑，并按照河北省文物部门技术人员的要求复原了那段被破坏的长城。该事件发生后，涞源县专门下发了《涞源县明长城保护工作的通告》，并组织乡镇及交通、公安、文旅、土地矿产等部门，在全县开展了长达3年的长城周边环境整治工作。

“各种选矿厂的房子被拆除了100多间，回填或者炸毁矿洞20多处，很多开矿设备被查处。同时，长城敌楼内的羊圈全部被迁出，长城恢复了本来面貌。”白石山景区管委会主任刘春阳回忆道。在这次大规模保护行动后，涞源还专门申请资金，开始对长城的加固尝试。

走进修葺后的乌字10号敌楼，三排甬道纵横相连，漫步其中宛若迷宫，时空穿越感油然而生。这是原始风貌保存最完好，也是最为精华的段落，涞源对明长城修复的第一次尝试，就在这里。

2009年，在发现涞源明长城乌龙沟段保存相对完好后，国家文物局文物保护与考古司（世界文化遗产司）专门拨款250万元，用于乌龙沟长城加固。2011年，涞源再次申请到200万元用于长城加固。

“从2013年7月份开始动工，一直到2015年4月份完工，我们对乌龙沟段进行了加固，特别是对10号敌楼进行了修葺尝试，效果不错。”安志敏说，“最近一次修葺加固是在2016年，河北省有关部门拨付了100万元，用于白石口长城的加固。”

“长城的修葺加固费用并不低，如果没有足够的政策和财力支持，长城长期保护工作仍然十分艰难。”安志敏忧心忡忡。

可喜的是，中共中央办公厅、国务院办公厅印发了《长城、大运河、长征国家文化公园建设方案》，明确要求根据文物和文化资源的整体布局、禀赋差异及周边人居环境、自然条件、配套设施等情况，重点建设管控保护、主题展示、文旅融合、传统利用四类主体功能区。同时，该文件提出将长城国家文化公园河北段纳入建设范围。更可喜的是，河北省委、省政府将涞源段长城列入第二批建设内容，要求到2023年完工。

涞源县委副书记贾伟斌介绍：“目前已经成立了涞源县长城国家文化公园建设领导小组，建设方案和规划正在制订中，按照河北省文旅厅、保定市文旅局的要求，未来将重点对乌龙沟长城30座敌台和浮图峪长城北楼台、南楼台段墙体，以及乌龙沟城堡进行抢修加固。同时，对白石口长城22座敌台、南城门墙体、北城门墙体进行抢修加固。”

更好的消息是，涞源明长城博物馆在2020年启动选址、论证、规划、设计等前期工作，涞源县长城文化协会也准备成立，长城文化知识讲座、高清宣传片和历史文化画册也在谋划中。

踏雪下山，回望崇山峻岭间连绵的城墙、挺拔的敌楼，它们在积雪的装点下更加壮丽，更显豪迈。历经400多年风吹雨打，迎来新契机的涞源段明长城，终将再展风华。

The Laiyuan Great Wall Keeps its Vigor through Wind and Frost

Di Zhiyong　Liu Hanning　Wang Dong

On the afternoon of December 24, 2019, in Zhujiaoshi Village of Wulonggou Town, Laiyuan County, Hebei Province, the Wulong River beside the village was glistening. There was still unmelted snow in distant mountains.

Our reporter was desperate for “the most beautiful Wild Great Wall”. Trekking pole in hand, the journalist followed An Zhimin, Director of Cultural Relics Protection Institute of Laiyuan County, to tramp on snow and search the city. They talked about the stories of the Great Wall protection in Laiyuan County.

“There are 71 watchtowers in the Wulonggou section of the Great Wall, only seven of which have been damaged. They are well-preserved like this after more than 400 years of war flames and natural erosion, which is rarely seen in the country.” An Zhimin said. Not all the sections of the Great Wall in Laiyuan County is as well preserved as the Wulonggou section. “Many sections of the Laiyuan Great Wall are traffic arteries. During the Anti-Japanese War, the watchtowers on the Great Wall, which occupied the commanding heights, were often the focus of contention between the enemy and our army. For example, the watchtowers on the Chajianling Great Wall was demolished from Building 4 to Building 27 during the Anti-Japanese War. Futuyu, Changjian’an and other sections of the Great Wall were also damaged due to the war.” An said. “There are a total of 269 watchtowers within the boundary of Laiyuan County, if they are all in good conditions, there is a good chance that they will be approved as world heritage sites."

In addition to natural erosion and war damage, man-made sabotage is also a major cause. Due to social and economic conditions, it has become a common phenomenon that some residents near the Great Wall removed the bricks from the ramparts when building houses. "In Dushancheng Village of Shuibao Town, the cornerstones of the Great Wall were used as the foundation of many old houses built in the 1920s and 1930s." An said. "In the 1970s, Baolai Highway was built and part of the Great Wall was demolished. Later, as the Laiyuan Steel Plant was built, some of the cornerstones of the Great Wall were also removed and used as the foundation of the plant."

In September 2002, An Zhimin, together with the staff of the Cultural Security Institute, conducted a general survey of the Great Wall. They discovered that many watchtowers in the well-preserved Wulonggou Great Wall were used by shepherds to make sheep pens. At that time, there were more copper and iron ores in Laiyuan County. Mining and building factories at the foot of the Great Wall posed a great threat to the preservation of the Great Wall.

It's never too late to mend. People's awareness of the Great Wall protection is constantly awakening.

In the 1950s, the Wulonggou section of the Ming Great Wall in Laiyuan County became a Hebei provincial cultural relic protection site. In 1999, Laiyuan County declared the Wulonggou Great Wall as a national protection site, which was approved in 2001. Since the survey of the Great Wall began in 2002, the local government has paid increasing attention to the preservation of the Great Wall as more problems have been discovered. "In 2002, we set up a team of 'the Great Wall protectors' and selected seven highly responsible villagers to strengthen the inspection and protection of the Great Wall." Jin Erleng, director of Laiyuan County Bureau of Tourism and Cultural Relics, said, "so far, the number of Great Wall protectors has grown to 21, reporting once a week about the protection work of the Great Wall."

The villagers' awareness of protection is also increasing. In 2004, the Futuyu Great Wall was excavated by 63 meters by a concentrating mill owner with a forklift. The case was reported by villagers, and hence the destroyer was sentenced. The damaged wall was restored according to the requirements of the technicians of Hebei Provincial Cultural Relics Department. After the incident, Laiyuan County issued a Notice on the Ming Great Wall Protection in Laiyuan County, and organized townships and departments like traffic, public security, cultural tourism, land and mineral resources to carry out a three-year-long surroundings improvement action for the Great Wall throughout the county.

"Over 100 houses in various concentrating mills have been demolished, over 20 mine caves have been backfilled or blown up, and many mining equipments have been checked and confiscated. At the same time, the sheep pens inside the watchtowers of the Great Wall were all moved out and restored to their original state." Recalls Liu Chunyang, director of the Baishi Mountain Scenic Area Management Committee. After the large-scale protection campaign, Laiyuan applied for funds to support the reinforcement of the Great Wall.

Walking into the renovated Wuzi No. 10 watchtower, it's clearly seen that three rows of corridors are connected vertically and horizontally. It is like walking in a maze, which helps creates a sense of space-time travel in people's mind. This place is considered as the most well-preserved and quintessential section of the Great Wall. The first attempt to restore the Ming Great Wall in Laiyuan started from here.

In 2009, the Cultural Relics Protection and Archaeology Department of the Ministry of Culture(the World Cultural Heritage Department)allocated RMB 2.5 million for the reinforcement of the Wulonggou Section of the Great Wall after the discovery of this relatively well-preserved section of the Ming Great Wall in Laiyuan. In 2011, Laiyuan got the fund of RMB 2 million for the reinforcement of the Great Wall.

"From the start of construction in July 2013 to completion in April 2015, we reinforced the Wulonggou section, and in particular tried to repair No. 10 watchtower, with good results." "The most recent renovation and reinforcement work were carried out in 2016. The relevant departments of Hebei Province allocated RMB 1 million for the reinforcement of the Baishikou Great Wall." An Zhimin said.

"The cost of repair and reinforcement of the Great Wall is not low, and without strong policy and financial support, the long-term preservation work of the Great Wall will still be very difficult." An Zhimin is full of worry.

Fortunately, the state has issued the Construction Plan for the Great Wall, the Grand Canal and the Long March National Cultural Park, which clearly states that "according to the overall layout of cultural relics and cultural resources, endowment differences, surrounding environment, natural conditions and infrastructure, four main functional areas, namely control and protection, theme exhibition, cultural tourism integration and traditional utilization, shall be constructed." The document also clearly included the Hebei section of the Great Wall National Cultural Park into the construction scope. What is more gratifying is that the Hebei Provincial Party Committee and the provincial government have listed the Laiyuan section of the Great Wall into the second batch of construction plan, with the requirement that the project be completed by 2023.

Jia Weibin, deputy secretary of the Laiyuan County Party Committee, said, "at present, the leading group for the construction of the Laiyuan Great Wall National Cultural Park has been established, and the construction plan are being formulated. According to the requirements of Hebei Provincial Department of Culture and Tourism and Baoding Municipal Bureau of Culture and Tourism, in the future, we will focus on the reinforcement of 30 watchtowers of the Wulonggou Great Wall, the ramparts of the north and south towers of the Futuyu Great Wall, as well as the Wulonggou Fortress. At the same time, the ramparts of 22 fortresses, the South Gate and the North Gate of the Baishikou Great Wall were reinforced."

The more encouraging news is that Laiyuan Great Wall Museum will start the preliminary work on site selection, demonstration, planning and design in 2020. The Great Wall Cultural Association of Laiyuan County is also ready to be established. Lectures on Great Wall culture, HD publicity videos and historical and cultural albums are also being planned.

Stepping down the mountain in the snow, we looked back at these rolling city walls and tall and straight watchtowers among the lofty mountains, which seemed to be more magnificent and heroic under the snow. After more than 400 years of wind and rain, the Ming Great Wall in Laiyuan, which has ushered in new opportunities, will eventually show its charm again.

为什么推荐保定的长城

张帆　赵顺利

作为人类历史上宏伟壮丽的建筑奇迹和无与伦比的历史文化景观，长城是我国现存规模宏大的文化遗产，更是中华民族的精神象征。2019年10月，国家正式启动长城国家文化公园建设项目。11月，河北省召开了推进长城国家文化公园建设工作会。对保定而言，长城国家文化公园的建设，有着极为重要的现实意义

涞源县石窝长城

和历史意义。为此，保定日报社专门联系中国长城学会会员、中国旅游未来研究会理事、河北大学旅游专业硕士研究生导师张帆，倾听其对保定长城的权威意见。

经过实地考察和文献调研，总结起来，保定境内的古长城具有如下特点。

其一，保定长城历史很悠久。

保定境内的长城是万里长城的重要组成部分。2012年，国家文物局宣布了基于6年的调查而统计出的中国境内历代长城总长度为21 196.18公里，而保定境内的长城总长度为247.545公里。

保定境内的长城主要分布于市域的西部地区，包括涞水、易县、涞源、唐县、阜平、曲阳、顺平、徐水。

保定境内现存最早的古长城主要是战国时代的中山国长城，稍后是战国时代的燕国长城（燕南长城），最后是明朝长城。

放眼全国，论各地长城历史之悠久，于公元前656年修建的、位于今河南省南阳市方城县的楚方城是长城之始，建于公元前555年的齐国平阴长城排在第二位，建于公元前369年的中山国长城则排在第三位。中山国长城在保定境内存有49.5公里，主要分布于唐县（约31.5公里）、顺平（约16.5公里）、涞源、曲阳等。

燕国修了北长城和南长城，燕南长城也称“易水长城”，修建于公元前334年，总长250多公里。其西起易县狼牙山东麓，向东经易县、徐水、容城、安新、雄县到文安、大城的子牙河西岸，现保定辖内分布于易县（约20.5公里）和徐水区（约38.9公里）。

保定境内涞源的明朝长城则修建于1573—1584年，全长150.48

公里，从东北到西南，经过涞水、易县、涞源、阜平、唐县。

从中山长城到明长城，保定长城修建的历史跨度达1954年。

其二，保定长城地位很重要。

保定长城位于太行山地及山前丘陵、台地和平原地带。其中明长城主要位于太行山区——我国地势的第二阶梯上。这个地带年等降水量为400毫米，基本上是中国的一条地理分界线，划分了半湿润气候区和半干旱气候区，也划分了游牧文明和农业文明。

中山长城为防御燕国和赵国所建，燕南长城为防御齐国和赵国所建，因此长城基本上是当时的诸侯国国界线。

保定明长城是明王朝北方防御体系的第三道防线，是“大边”“二边”之后的“内边”，属于内长城，是从内蒙古、山西到河北之间长城墙体的第四道，是明朝中后期统治者为加强京师防御能力而增修的，由增设的真保镇管辖，是京师和中原地区的最后一道防线。著名的“内三关”中的紫荆关、倒马关坐落在保定境内。

其三，保定长城体系很独特。

保定是全中国和全世界唯一集合了山地长城、平原河堤长城、平原地下长城和水系长城的地区。

中山长城和明长城基本布局在山地、丘陵；燕南长城主要布局在平原，是沿南易水河岸构筑的河堤长城。

位于雄县、霸州、文安、永清境内，修建于北宋“雍熙北伐”（986）后，用于抗辽的边关地下战道被称为“地下长城”。地道分布区域东西长65公里，南北宽65公里，总面积达4225平方公里。

几乎在修建地下战道的同期，北宋于987年开始修筑水长城，西起保州西塘泊（今府河、清苑河），东至沧州泥沽海口（今天津军粮城泥沽村），全长近千里。绵亘7座军州的水长城范围包括保州（今保定）、雄州、霸州、瀛州（今河间）、莫州（今任丘北）、沧州、定州。水长城沿途汇集了河流19条、淀泊30个。其全线分为8个区段，设置堡垒26座、军铺125个，驻士兵3000余人，还有战舰100余艘往来巡警。

其四，保定长城风貌很古朴。

保定境内的战国、明朝等各长城均保持了原生态的自然古朴风貌，是目前全国少数没有经过当代人工修缮再建的长城。尤其是乌龙沟—浮图峪段长城保存的完好度，全国少见。涞源县120公里明长城全线均被列入全国重点文物保护单位，这在全国是非常罕见的。因为侧重于保护，保定也是目前拥有优质长城文化资源却没有开发长城旅游景区的地区。

其五，保定长城抗战历史很辉煌。

中国的长城抗战发生在两个时段和两个区域。

一个是1933年发生在山海关、义院口、冷口、喜峰口、古北口等燕山地区明长城沿线的对日抗战，主力部队是东北军、西北军和中央军。

另一个是1937—1945年发生在太行山长城沿线的对日抗战，参战部队有中央军、晋绥军和八路军。著名战役有平型关战役、忻口会战、雁门关伏击战、娘子关战役、阳明堡大捷、雁宿崖战斗、黄土岭战斗、东团堡战斗、大茂山保卫战等，其中雁宿崖战斗、黄土岭战斗、东团堡战斗、大茂山保卫战及平型关战役的一部分发生在保定长城沿线地区。保定长城沿线还是著名的中国共产党领导的晋察冀抗日根据地核心区域和指挥机关所在，是八路军发动的百团大战的重要战场。著名的国际主义战士白求恩、柯

棣华就曾战斗在保定长城沿线并牺牲于此，因此这里还是“白求恩国际主义精神”的诞生处。

长城春天

The Reasons for Recommending the Great Wall in Baoding

Zhang Fan Zhao Shunli

As a magnificent architectural miracle and incomparable historical and cultural landscape in human history, the Great Wall is a huge cultural heritage in China, and a spiritual symbol of the Chinese nation as well. In October 2019, the government officially launched a project for the construction of the Great Wall National Cultural Park. In November, a meeting was held in Hebei Province to promote the construction of the Great Wall National Cultural Park. For Baoding, it is of great practical and historical significance. To this end, our newspaper office contacted Zhang Fan, a member of China Great Wall Institution, director of China Tourism Future Research Association, and tutor for graduate students majoring in tourism at Hebei University, to seek expert advice on the Great Wall in Baoding.

After the field investigation and document research, it is found that the ancient Great Wall in Baoding has the following characteristics.

First, the Baoding Great Wall has a long history.

The Great Wall in Baoding is an important part of the Great Wall. After 6 years of investigation, the State Administration of Cultural Heritage announced that the total length of the Great Wall in China was 21,196.18 kilometers, while the total length in Baoding section was 247.545 kilometers.

The Great Wall in Baoding is mainly distributed in the western part of the city, including Laishui, Yixian, Laiyuan, Tangxian, Fuping, Quyang, Shunping and Xushui.

The earliest existing Ancient Great Wall in Baoding is the Great Wall of Zhongshan State in the Warring States Period, followed by the Great Wall of Yan state in the same period, and finally the Great Wall of the Ming Dynasty.

In the long history of the Great Wall across the country, Chu Fangcheng(the square-shaped walled city located in Chu State), which was built in 656 BC and located in Fangcheng county of Nanyang City, Henan Province, is the beginning of the Great Wall. The Pingyin Great Wall(also named Qi Great Wall in Shangdong Province)of Qi State, built in 555 BC, ranks second, and the Zhongshan Great Wall, built in 369 BC, ranks third. The total length of the Zhongshan Great Wall in Baoding is 49.5 kilometers, mainly distributed in Tangxian(about 31.5 kilometers in length), Shunping (about 16.5 kilometers in length), Laiyuan, Quyang and other counties.

Yan State built the North and the South Great Wall. The Great Wall in the south of Yan State, also known as the Yishui Great Wall, was built with a total length of more than 250 kilometers in 334 BC. It stretches from the eastern foot of Langya Mountain in Yixian County in the west and runs eastward through Yixian, Xushui, Rongcheng, Anxin and Xiongxian to the west bank of the Ziya River in Wen'an and Dacheng. It is now distributed in Yixian(about 20.5 kilometers in length) and Xushui(38.9 kilometers in length) within the jurisdiction of Baoding.

The Ming Great Wall in Laiyuan of Baoding, was built with a total length of 150.48 kilometers from 1573 to 1584. It runs from northeast to southwest through many places including Laishui, Yixian, Laiyuan, Fuping and Tangxian.

From the Zhongshan Great Wall to the Ming Great Wall, the construction of the Great Wall stretches over 1954 years in history.

Second, the Baoding Great Wall has a vital position.

It is located in Taihang Mountain area, lower terrace, mesa and plains. The Great Wall of the Ming Dynasty is mainly located in Taihang Mountain area, the second step of China's terrain. This zone, which has an annual average precipitation of 400 millimeters, is essentially a geographic dividing line between China's semi-humid and semi-arid climates, as well as the line between nomadic and agricultural civilizations.

The Zhongshan Great Wall was built to defend Yan and Zhao States, and the Yannan Great Wall was built to defend Qi and Zhao States. Therefore, the

Great Wall was basically the boundary line of the vassal states at that time.

The northern defense system of the Ming Dynasty had three defense lines. The Ming Great Wall in Baoding is the third defense line, which belongs to the Inner Great Wall. It is the fourth wall of the Great Wall between Inner Mongolia, Shanxi and Hebei. It was built in the mid- and late Ming Dynasty to strengthen the defense capability of the capital. It was then under the jurisdiction of Zhenbao Town and served as the last defense line between the capital and the Central Plain area. The famous "Three Inner Passes" are Juyongguan, Zijingguan, Daomaguan, among which Zijingguan and Daomaguan are located in Baoding.

Third, the Baoding Great Wall has a unique system.

Baoding is the only area that gathers mountain great wall, plain river embankment great wall, plain underground great wall and drainage great wall in China and the world.

The Zhongshan Great Wall and the Ming Great Wall are basically laid out in mountains and hills; The Yannan Great Wall is mainly deployed in a plain as the river embankment of the South Yishui River.

Located in Xiongxian, Bazhou, Wen'an, and Yongqing, it was built after the "Northern Expedition in the Period of Yongxi"(986 AD)in the Northern Song Dynasty. The underground tunnel in the frontier pass, which was used to resist the Liao army, was called the "Underground Great Wall". The tunnel area is 65 kilometers long from east to west, 65 kilometers wide from north to south, with a total area of 4,225 square kilometers.

Almost at the same time as the construction of the underground tunnel, the Northern Song Dynasty began to build the Great Wall in water system in 987 AD, starting from Xitangbo in Baozhou City(today's Fuhe and Qingyuan River)in the west and ending at Nigu Haikou in Cangzhou (today's Nigu Village, the city of military provision in Tianjin)in the east, with a total length of nearly 1,000 li(one li refers to about one third of an English mile and now has a standard length of a half-kilometer). The Great Wall in river system stretches across seven military prefectures including Baozhou(Baoding), Xiongzhou, Bazhou, Yingzhou(Hejian), Mozhou(Renqiubei), Cangzhou and Dingzhou. Along the Great Wall in river system, there are 19 rivers and 30 lakes. The whole line is divided into 8 sections, with 26 forts, 125 courier stations for military use, over 3,000 soldiers, and 100 warships for patrol.

Fourth, the Baoding Great Wall is characterized by primitive simplicity.

The Great Wall built during the Warring States Period, Ming Dynasty and other dynasties in Baoding have kept its original natural and primitive style. It is currently one of the few Great Walls in the country that has not been renovated by people nowadays. Especially the Wulonggou-Futuyu section of the Great Wall is well preserved, which is rarely seen in the country. The entire 120-kilometer Ming Great Wall in Laiyuan county is listed as a national key cultural relics protection unit, which is the only one in the country. Due to its focus on protection, Baoding is also an area that embraces high-quality cultural resources of the Great Wall, but has not fully exploited the Great Wall tourist attractions.

Fifth, the Baoding Great Wall witnessed glories of Chinese army in the Anti-Japanese war.

The Anti-Japanese war along the Great Wall took place in two periods and two regions.

One is the Anti-Japanese War that occurred along the Ming Great Wall in Shanhaiguan, Yiyuankou, Lengkou, Xifengkou, Gubeikou and other Yanshan areas in 1933. The main forces in this war are the Northeast Army, the Northwest Army and the Central Army.

The other is the Anti-Japanese War that took place along the Great Wall in Taihang Mountain area from 1937 to 1945. The troops involved were the Central Army, the Jin-Sui Army and the Eighth Route Army. The famous battles include Pingxingguan Battle, Xinkou Battle, Yanmenguan Battle, Niangziguan Battle, the Great Victory of Yangmingbao, Yansuya-Huangtuling Battle, Dongtuanbao Battle, and the Defense Battle of Damao Mountain. Among them, Yansuya-Huangtuling Battle, Dongtuanbao Battle, the Defense Battle of Damao Mountain, and Pingxingguan Battle took place along the Baoding Great Wall. Areas along the Great Wall in Baoding was the core of the famous Jin-Cha-Ji Anti-Japanese Military Region led by the Communist Party of China. It was also the seat of its headquarters and the main battlefield of the Hundred-Regiment Battle launched by the Eighth Route Army. Bethune and Ke Lihua, famous internationalist soldiers, once fought and died along the Baoding Great Wall. Therefore, it is considered as the birthplace of Bethune's spirit of internationalism.

插箭岭下有人家

梁晓冬　孟海英　王栋　张保林

插箭岭下的这个小村，四面环山，三面围城。

初去涞源，初见长城，是20多年前的一个暮春。远处起伏攀升的山脊上，残墙断续，时现楼台；山坡尚未返青，凸显一窝窝山桃花摇曳着火红，似灵动的红狐，令人遐想着“飞狐县”的来由。

史载，位于太行山、燕山、恒山三山交汇处的涞源，是宋辽时期的主战场。

207国道弯弯绕绕穿过一片破败的房舍，同车人说这就是插箭岭。当年杨六郎同辽军在倒马关大战，杨六郎与辽将比箭划界，从倒马关一箭射到如今的插箭岭，逼退辽军30余里，大胜。

箭，贯穿着中国民间几千年的英雄史——后羿落九日，李广没石棱，薛仁贵定天山，杨六郎得插箭岭。

暮冬，胸怀壮烈，攀爬插箭岭村南的长城。眼前这段长城墙体坍塌，山脊如刃，石块犬牙交错,只得踩着石棱跃进，两侧都是陡坡。冒虚汗、看远方，长城依山盘绕很是诱人，但脚下艰险，只得铩羽而归。“不到长城非好汉”是说此处?

山脚处，疏林冷落，枯雪无神。村委会副主任火红强说，这

插箭岭长城

原是插箭岭城堡的南门，前几年国道改建时拆了。与早年相比，眼前的大道确实宽敞，几乎没有弯道。

插箭岭得名于宋辽，成制在明朝。《河北省志·长城志》记载，现存的长城始建于明弘治三年（1490），“插箭岭口山狭路峭，北通紫荆关，南达倒马关”。其后几十年不断增修敌台、马面、烽火台、挡马墙，勾连南北直至体系完整。插箭岭关堡有南、中、北三门，为“重门堡城”，据考，应建于更早的明景泰年间。

明嘉靖三十二年（1553），俺答汗攻进大同，向紫荆关进攻，曾在插箭岭与明军发生战斗。俺答汗是当时蒙古土默特部首领。说来笑话，自明嘉靖二十九年（1550）的“庚戌之变”，俺答汗连年与明开战，原因竟是怨恨明政府不开放边贸。

据插箭岭当地文史部门的同志说，抗战时期，这里为游击区，没有大的战役。

插箭岭关堡的中门、北门还有门洞。中门洞浑身是石材，石条墙体粗糙，石板路面光滑。《河北省志·长城志》载，“重门堡城”最多时拥兵3000多人。中门距南门、北门距离均等，想来，若战事有失，中门可居中调度，攻守有据。今日过中门，仍恍若“车辚辚，马萧萧，行人弓箭各在腰”。

出门洞又是一片天地，旧时关堡已成百姓家。曲径多是石卵、石板路，新建、翻新的农舍比比皆是红顶白墙，每家的电表箱都整齐划一装在院墙外，角角落落都是崭新的高杆路灯。

插箭岭紧靠AAAAA级景区白石山。火红强说，这几年，政府提供低息贷款，全村200多户人家（500多人）有30%办起农家乐。这里夏季气候凉爽，农家乐接待的多是“避暑团”，收益不错。余下村民去景区卖山货，村里几乎没闲人。过了旅游旺季，村民再外出打短工，基本长年有收入。

地理和气候原因，使插箭岭区域耕地少而薄。

一座二层小楼对着一排平房，院门大开，迎门端坐一个大雪人，黑煤球点睛，鼻子是带粒儿的玉米棒，小嘴又是煤球，塑料袋变身黄丝巾，俏皮，可爱，让人不禁走进院里。

杨玉芝闻声迎出，没有丝毫陌生感。问她盖新楼是否要开农家乐，她说，老伴儿辛辛苦苦把什么都弄好了，去年因一场大病走了，现在她还没精力开农家乐。大儿子两口子在外地工作，二儿子在外打工。等开春，在院子种菜，平房顶上垫土也种上菜。

言语间，杨玉芝面带微笑，语气平和。她说，雪人是她亲手堆的。

新戏台连着北门洞，戏台两侧对联大书：一箭得名以岭为界分胡汉；千年有声凭台演史唱古今。

《宋史》有关杨业（老令公）的最终记载是与辽交战兵败被俘，绝食三日而亡；除了儿子杨延昭之外，并没有涉及其他子嗣的记录。自明后，杨家将的形象在各种民间艺术载体中日益丰满多样，传说"传说"的是民心的力量，其中也有统治者的需要助推。

每年都有地方剧种来插箭岭再现"杨六郎"的故事，而国粹京剧中"杨四郎"的故事也是家喻户晓。"金沙滩杀得杨家好不悲哀"，杨四郎被困番邦十五载，闻知佘太君随杨六郎挂帅出征，夜奔宋营。戏中——

佘太君：一见娇儿泪满腮……

杨四郎：千拜万拜也折不过儿的罪来……十五载……每年花开儿的心不开……

佘太君：……夫妻恩爱不恩爱？公主贤才不贤才？都是家里的话儿。

插箭岭长城关堡

插箭岭长城

催人泪下的故事流传大江南北，广东一带还有潮剧版的《四郎探母》。按情理，四郎探母之地离插箭岭不太远。

孝，是国人的软肋。据说《四郎探母》被清朝统治者欣赏，是因突出了“孝”弱化了“忠”，能缓解满汉矛盾。哪知，百姓自有情怀。

作家蒋勋回忆，当时军中剧团推出新编《四郎探母》：拜完之后，儿子从袖中拿出一卷东西递给母亲，说“这是敌营的地图，母亲可率领大军，一举歼灭辽邦”，正热泪涟涟的老兵们见此顿时拂袖而去。为了政治理由而粗暴改动一出长久在人们心中形成力量的戏，其实是愚蠢的。

插箭岭村口的碑文铭刻：……现有长城40公里，敌台53座、城堡2座、烽火台2座……

有人把长城简单看成古代军事系统防御工程体系，仅存游玩

插箭岭长城

价值。

有人说，修建长城之初，不仅带动了北方经济的发展，在其后的岁月中还持续促进了中华民族的凝聚和融合。

更有人说，长城像一部中国2000多年历史的百科全书，包含着许多已知和未知。

48年前，京原铁路穿越重重峻岭经涞源一路向西；1000年前，涞源尽处皆是“胡地”；几十年来，108、112、207国道陆续贯穿涞源全境；这几年，荣乌、张石、太行山高速路凌驾拒马源、涞水源、易水源，跃上太行山、燕山、恒山。

历史有沉香，长城期待人们走近走进、感知感悟。长城老了，需要唤醒、呵护，与新时代同频共振。

（历史文化顾问：河北大学博物馆副馆长、教授李文龙）

A Village at the Foot of Chajianling

Liang Xiaodong Meng Haiying Wang Dong Zhang Baolin

The small village at the bottom of Chajianling(Arrow Mountain Ridge) is surrounded by mountains and besieged by cities on three sides.

In a late spring of over 20 years ago, I went to Laiyuan County in Hebei Province, where I saw the Great Wall for the first time. On the ridge that rises and falls in the distance, the residual wall is intermittent, and the tower appears occasionally; The hillside has not yet turned verdant while bunches of peach blossoms are swaying with flaming red, just like nimble red foxes, which reminds people of the origin about “Feihu(Flying Fox)County”.

According to historical records, Laiyuan county, located at the intersection of Taihang mountain, Yan mountain and Heng mountain, was the main battlefield in the Song and Liao dynasties.

Driving along the National Highway 207, we went through a group of dilapidated houses. Our companion said that was Chajianling, where the generals of the Yang family had a big battle with the Liao army here. It is where Yang Liulang delimited the border with the Liao army by shooting arrows. In here, Yang Liulang shot an arrow westward from Daomaguan, forcing the Liao army to retreat for 30 li(one li refers to about one third of an English mile and now has a standard length of a half-kilometer), and finally won a big victory.

Arrows have played a vital role in the folklore history of heroes over thousands of years in China. Stories like Hou Yi who shot down nine suns, Li Guang who shot an arrow deeply into a stone, Xue Rengui who conquered Tianshan Mountain with three arrows and Yang Liulang who performed archery in the Chajianling Ridge are all household tales.

In deep winter, one may be in great awe when climbing the Great Wall in the south of the Chajianling Village. The section of Great Wall in front of our eyes almost has nothing left but relics —the wall has collapsed, the blade-like ridges and scattered rocks around the site left travelers with no other option but to hop forward, with a danger of falling off the steep slopes at both sides. Sweating, I had to return given the danger under my feet despite the temptation of the distant views of the Great Wall running along the winding mountains. Isn't the saying "one who fails to reach the Great Wall is not a true man" more apt when applied to this section?

At the foot of the mountain were lonely, sparse woods and lifeless, melting snow. Huo Hongqiang, deputy director of the Villagers' Committee, said that this place was originally the south gate of the Chajianling Fort, which was dismantled a few years ago when a national road was rebuilt. Compared with a few years ago, the newly built road is indeed broader and with almost no bend.

Chajianling gained its name during the Song and Liao period and was officially established in the Ming Dynasty. According to *Hebei Province chronicles: the Great Wall Volume*, the existing Great Wall was originally built in the third year of Emperor Hongzhi of the Ming Dynasty(1490), and "the Chajianling Pass surrounded by steep slopes connects the Zijingguan in the north and Daomaguan in the south". The continuous construction of watchtowers, buttresses, beacon towers and horse-fending walls in dozens of subsequent years enabled a connection from the south to the north until the system was completed. The Chajianling Fort has three gates, the south, middle and north gates, which is why it is called a "multi-gate fort". According to research, the fort should have been built during the reign of Emperor Jingtai of the Ming Dynasty, an earlier time than previously expected.

"In the 32nd year of Emperor Jiajing of Ming(1553), Altan Khan moved into Datong City and marched towards Zijingguan. A battle took place at

Chajianling." Altan Khan was Mongol tribal leader of Tümed at the time. It still seems like a joke that the endless wars waged by Altan Khan against the Ming Dynasty since the 29th year of Emperor Jiajing of Ming(historically referred to as the "Change of Gengxu")were actually due to his resentment against the Ming government's refusal to open border trade.

According to people working in the local Cultural and Historical Department, it was a guerrilla zone without major battles during the Anti-Japanese War.

Today, I passed the Middle Gate. I seemed to see "rattling carts, neighing horses and pedestrians with an arrow in waist" in a trance.

The Middle Gate and the North Gate still have doorways. The middle gate is built with stone, with rugged stone walls and smooth slate road. As recorded in *Hebei Province Annals: the Great Wall Volume*, a multi-gate fort had more than 3,000 troops at its peak. The Middle Gate is equal in distance from the South Gate and the North Gate. If the war is lost, the Middle Gate can be arranged in the middle to attack and defend.

Out of the gate, you may see a different world. The ancient passes and forts have turned to be the home of local residents. The winding paths are paved with stone pebbles and stone slabs. Newly built and renovated farmhouses are decorated with red roofs and white walls. Each electricity meter box is neatly arranged outside the courtyard, and each corner is covered with brand-new high-pole street lamps.

Chajianling is close to Baishi Mountain, which is a 5A scenic spot. Huo Hongqiang said that in recent years, the government provided low-interest loans, and 30% of more than 200 households(more than 500 people)in the village set up agritainment hotels .

It is cool here in summer. Therefore, most agritainment hotels accommodate "summer vacation groups", and their income is good. The rest of villagers go to the scenic spot to sell mountain products, and there are almost no idlers in the village. After the peak tourist season, villagers usually go out to work as short-term workers, and they basically have annual income.

Due to geographical position and climate, the cultivated land in Chajianling is small and infertile.

A two-story building faced to a row of bungalows. The door was opened. A big snowman was sitting inside the door, eyes and mouth made of black coalballs, nose made of a corncob, and a yellow scarf made of a plastic bag. What a smart and cute snowman! I could not help walking into the courtyard.

Yang Yuzhi heard my voice, and came out. Asked if she would build a farmhouse for agritainment activities, she said her husband died after everything got ready last year, so she has no energy to start an agritainment hotel now. Her eldest son and his wife, and her second-born son all worked off the hometown. Into spring, she will grow vegetables in the yard and on the top of the bungalow.

In our talk, Yang Yuzhi smiled and spoke in a peaceful tone. She said that the snowman was made by herself.

The new drama stage is connected with the North Gate. The couplets on both sides of the stage say: The Wall divided Hu and Han; dramas are performed about the past and the present.

The final record about Yang Ye(Lao Ling Gong) in the *History of Song* is that Yang was captured in a battle with Liao army and died on hunger strike three days later. Except his son Yang Yanzhao, there is no record of his other offspring. From the Ming Dynasty, the image of "generals of the Yang family" became full and diversified in various folk carriers. The legend represented popular sentiments, and also the aspiration of rulers.

Every year, local drama teams came to Chajianling to perform "Yang Liulang". Compared with "Yang Silang" in Beijing Opera, "Yang Liulang" is slightly weak. "The Jinshatan War was devastating for the Yang family." Yang Silang(Yang Yanhui, Emperor's son-in-law of Liao State)is trapped in Liao State for 15 years. Upon hearing that Taijun She follows Yang Liulang in an expedition to Liao, Yang Silang rushes to the camp of Song. Here is the scene in the opera:

Taijun She: I burst into tears upon seeing my beloved son...Yang Silang: I kowtow and kowtow. But this cannot counteract my sin...for fifteen years...flowers blossomed every year, while I never felt happy...Taijun She: Do you love each other? Is your wife considerate or not? All family stuff...

The touching story is spread across the country. In Guangdong, there is a

Chaozhou opera version of *Silang Visits His Mother*. It is speculated that the site where Silang visited his mother is not far from Chajianling.

Filial piety is a soft part in the heart of Chinese people. It is said that *Silang Visits His Mother* was appreciated by the rulers of the Qing Dynasty because it highlighted filial piety and weakened loyalty, so it could alleviate the contradiction between Manchu and Han. In fact, people had their own sentiments.

As the writer Jiang Xun recalled, a military opera troupe launched a new edition of *Silang Visits His Mother*: after kowtow, the son takes out a scroll from his sleeve and handed it to his mother, saying, "This is a map of the enemy barrack. You can lead your army to destroy Liao State." Hearing this, tearful soldiers all stormed out of the room. It is foolish to alter a play that has long shaped power in people's mind only for political reasons.

The monumental inscription at the entrance to Chajianling Village records that there were 40-kilometer-long Great Wall, 53 watchtowers, 2 forts and 2 beacon towers …

Some people simply regard the Great Wall as the defensive engineering system of ancient military affairs, which is only suitable for sightseeing.

Some people say that the construction of the Great Wall promoted the development of the northern economy at the beginning, and will continue to promote the cohesion and integration of the Chinese nation in the following years.

Some people even say that the Great Wall is like an encyclopedia with the Chinese history of more than 2,000 years, which contains many known and unknown things.

Forty eight years ago, Jingyuan Railway crossed many steep mountains and went all the way to the west through Laiyuan; One thousand years ago, Laiyuan County belonged to the Hu people; For decades, National Highways 108, 112 and 207 have been running through the entire territory of Laiyuan County; In recent years, Rongwu, Zhangshi and Taihang Mountain Expressways have surpassed the three water sources, namely, Juma Yuan, Laishui Yuan and Yishui Yuan, and leaped over Taihang Mountain, Yan Mountain and Heng Mountain.

History has a profound fragrance. The Great Wall expects people to approach it and perceive it. The Great Wall is old. He needs to be awaken and cared so as to resonate with the new era. He is looking forward to his present life.

(The consultant on history and culture: Professor Li Wenlong, deputy curator of Hebei University Museum)

插箭岭长城

保定长城国家文化公园建设中的几个辩证关系

张帆

长城、大运河、长征三大国家文化公园建设，是新中国成立以来，由国家提出并实施的规格与规模都空前的重大国家公共文化工程，其对传承和弘扬优秀中华文化、树立社会主义核心价值观、促进中华民族伟大复兴的重要性不言而喻。因此，长城国家文化公园建设这一世纪性的伟大工程，在具体工作实践中，应注意处理好以下五个关系。

第一，宏观与微观的关系。

中共中央办公厅、国务院办公厅印发的《长城、大运河、长征国家文化公园建设方案》，已就公园建设的指导思想、建设原则、建设范围、建设内容、建设目标、主要任务及要推进的五项基础工程做出框架性部署和原则要求。将中央的精神与保定实际相结合，忠实地贯彻中央的总方针和总体安排，而又因地制宜、因时制宜地把保定段的长城文化公园建设成为带有鲜明的保定特色和特征的公园，从而使其具有特殊的魅力、影响力和感召力，提高入园群众、游客对保定长城文化的领受力、传播力，是保定市的重要任务和努力方向。

针对保定长城旅游尚未起步、长城文化资源发掘和宣传不足、长城知名度不彰的状态，在中央明确的保护传承、研究发掘、环境配套、文旅融合、数字再现五大工程基础上，保定因地制宜地增加宣传教育工程内容，就是应有之义。

第二，共性与个性的关系。

万里长城作为历史上多个朝代修建的国家军事防御工程体系，纵向跨越战国、秦、汉、晋、北朝、隋、唐、宋（金、辽、西夏）、明、清的几乎整个中国近古史，修建时间达2300余年；横向跨越东西向的新疆到黑龙江，南北向的内蒙古至湖南，地域囊括了大半个中国的15个省、区、市。

长城作为防御体系，其建筑形态包括墙、关、城、障、堡、燧、楼、台、墩、堑、壕等，在总体上具有共性和一般特征。但是，各地长城所处地域的区位地理、自然风貌、生态环境、历史文化、人文风情、人口聚落、民族构成、戍守形式、道路交通等是有差别的、有个性的。

因此，各地需要在共性中发掘个性，在大长城文化中发掘和凸显地域文化特色，在长城整体建筑一般结构体系中找到不一般的亮点并着力宣传，以在长城文化旅游开发中作为卖点。

具体到保定，作为太行山长城、内长城和“内三关”之二所在地，作为长城抗战的重要战场，作为国内少有的与清西陵、野三坡、白石山等著名文化与自然（地质）遗产资源组合之地，并拥有天生桥、古北岳等绿色生态文化资源与城南庄、和家庄等红色文化资源聚合之优势，保定长城文化公园中的文旅融合工程理应具有自己的个性和独特魅力。

第三，保护与利用的关系。

在严格保护长城这一中华民族重要的文化遗产前提下，适度、科学、有序地利用长城资源，建设长城主体文化景区和文旅融合区，开发文物的旅游功能，让文物活起来，让文化遗产为当代和今后的文化建设服务、为经济社会发展服务，让沿线人民受益，发挥好长城精神对人民群众的教化功能，面向国际发挥中华文化展示窗口功能，是中央实施长城国家文化公园建设工程的基本立意和宗旨。

因此，让沉睡上千年、数百年的保定长城走向世界，就是这次保定段长城文化公园建设工程的重点与核心任务。

第四，传承与创新的关系。

建设长城文化公园，传承无疑是最基本的诉求。这包括物质形态的传承，即尽最大努力保存延续长城构筑物寿命；意识形态的传承，即着力挖掘和弘扬长城所蕴含、代表的文化内涵与文化精神。

但仅有传承是不够的，必须在尊重和坚守传统的基础上，探索长城本体保护、维修、监控等技术手段的必要创新，长城文化内涵的创新诠释和创新表达，以适应互联网时代、移动媒体时代和新新人类生活方式及文化消费习惯的改变。即便建设长城主体文化景区、景点，也要考虑文旅项目和文旅产品的创新，不然在全国长城沿线已辟有八达岭、山海关、嘉峪关、居庸关、金山岭、司马台、慕田峪、九门口、黄崖关、雁门关、镇北台、玉门关等90多个景区、景点，已建有山海关、八达岭、居庸关、黄崖关、嘉峪关等多个长城博物馆并还要规划在金山岭、大境门、崇礼等地新建长城主题文化博物馆的形势下，居后发者位置的保定长城文化景区建设，在资源整合、功能定位、主打产品、文博场馆、旅游线路、衍生文创、表达形式等方面的创新开发任务是艰巨的，也是不容回避的。

第五，本体与环境的关系。

不仅是指长城本体与所在地自然生态的关系，更是指长城与周边的人居社区、产业群落、基础设施等方面的关系。

长城沿线传统历史村落所承载的民俗文化、人文风情、建筑形态等是长城文化生态体系的重要组成部分，是特色长城文化旅游产品开发所倚赖的重要资源，是长城区域历史文脉不可割舍的纽带，是远行的长城守关人后裔难忘的乡愁，是闻名而来的长城访客体验地道乡情民俗的载体和媒介。

因此，保护好保定长城周边现存的优良自然与人文两种生态环境也是科学建设长城文化公园的重要任务，是体现保定长城文化公园的特色、个性与优势所在。

Dialectical Relations: The Construction of the Great Wall National Cultural Park in Baoding

Zhang Fan

Since the founding of People's Republic of China, the construction of the Great Wall, the Grand Canal and the Long March National Cultural Parks, which is proposed and implemented by the government, has been a major national cultural project with unprecedented specifications and scale. It is of great significance to inherit and carry forward the grand Chinese culture, establish the socialist core values and promote the great rejuvenation of the Chinese nation. Therefore, the construction of the Great Wall National Cultural Park, a great project of the century, should focus on the following five relationships in actual work practice.

First, the relationship between macrocosm and microcosm.

The Construction Plan for the Great Wall,the Grand Canal and the Long March National Cultural Park, issued by the CPC Central Committee and the State Council, has made the overall framework and principles on the following aspects: guiding ideology, construction principles, construction scope, construction content, construction objectives, main tasks and five basic projects to be promoted. We should integrate the spirit of the Central Committee into the actual situation of Baoding, and faithfully implement the general policy and arrangement of the Central Committee. Meanwhile, the Great Wall Cultural Park in Baoding will be built into a park with distinctive Baoding characteristics according to local conditions. Therefore, it has a special charm, influence and appeal, and it is an important task and future direction for Baoding City to improve the acceptance and dissemination of the Great Wall culture to the visitors.

Considering that the Great Wall Tourism in Baoding has not yet started, the cultural resources of the Great Wall are not fully explored and publicized, and its popularity has yet to be boosted, Baoding should enrich the content of publicity and education project according to local conditions on the basis of five projects. These projects are clearly defined by the central government, namely, protection and inheritance, research and excavation, supporting environment, culture and tourism integration, and digital reproduction.

Second, the relationship between generality and individuality.

As a national military defense system built in many dynasties in history, the Great Wall spans nearly the entire ancient Chinese history—the Warring States Period, Qin Dynasty, Han Dynasty, Jin Dynasty, Northern Dynasty, Sui Dynasty, Tang Dynasty, Song Dynasty(Jin, Liao, Xixia), Ming and Qing Dynasties, with a construction time of more than 2,300 years. It stretches eastward from Xinjiang to Heilongjiang, and runs southward from Inner Mongolia to Hunan, covering more than half area of China including 15 provinces, autonomous regions and cities.

As a defense system, the architectural forms of the Great Wall include rampart, pass, city, barrier, castle, beacon, tower, platform, mound, moat and trench, which shows similar features on the whole. However, the Great Wall has unique characteristics in many aspects: geographical location, natural features, ecological environment, history and culture, human customs, population settlement, ethnic composition, garrison form, road traffic, etc.

Therefore, all regions need to explore individuality in generality, explore and manifest the characteristics of regional culture in the Great Wall culture, discover the unusual highlights in the general structural system of the Great Wall architecture, and make great efforts to publicize them, so as to create a selling point in the Great Wall cultural tourism development.

Baoding is a crucial place where the Great Wall of Taihang Mountain, the Inner Great Wall and two of the Inner Three Passes are located. As an important battlefield with the Great Wall as a barrier to resist Japanese invaders, and a rare place which integrates world-class cultural and natural (geological)heritage resources such as Xiling(the Western Qing Tombs),

Ye'sanpo and Baishi Mountain, and integrates national green ecological cultural resources such as Tianshengqiao, Gubeiyue and Motianling, and red cultural resources such as Chengnanzhuang and Hejiazhuang. The cultural tourism integration project in Baoding Great Wall Cultural Park should have its own personality and unique charm.

Third, the relationship between protection and utilization.

Under the premise of strictly protecting the Great Wall—an important cultural heritage of the Chinese nation, we can utilize the Great Wall in an appropriate, scientific and orderly manner, and then build the main cultural scenic area and cultural tourism integration area of the Great Wall. In addition, we can develop the tourism function of cultural relics and make cultural relics alive, which could make the cultural heritage serve the present and future cultural construction, promote the economic and social development, and benefit the residents around the Great Wall. The basic intention and purpose of constructing the Great Wall National Cultural Park are to perform the educational function of the Great Wall Spirit and to display Chinese culture to the world.

Therefore, awakening the Great Wall in Baoding, which has slept for hundreds and thousands of years, and making it develop globally are the core tasks for constructing the Great Wall Cultural Park in Baoding.

Fourth, the relationship between inheritance and innovation.

To build the Great Wall Cultural Park, inheritance is undoubtedly the most basic requirement. This includes the inheritance of the Great Wall as a tangible heritage, that is, the preservation of the Great Wall and the extension of its life span; the inheritance of ideology, which refers to excavating and carrying forward the cultural connotation and spirit represented by the Great Wall.

However, only inheritance is not enough. On the basis of respecting and adhering to tradition, we must explore essential innovations in the protection, maintenance, monitoring and other technical means of the Great Wall, and excavate the innovative interpretation and expression of the cultural connotation about the Great Wall, so as to adapt to the changes of the Internet age, the mobile media era, the lifestyle of X-generation and the habits of cultural consumption. In the course of constructing the main cultural scenic areas of the Great Wall, innovations in projects and products of culture and tourism should be considered. Otherwise, in the context that more than 90 scenic spots and areas, such as Badaling, Shanhaiguan, Jiayuguan, Juyongguan, Jinshanling, Simatai, Mutianyu, Jiumenkou, Huangyaguan, Yanmenguan, Zhenbeitai and Yumenguan, have been built along the Great Wall; many Great Wall Museums such as Shanhaiguan, Badaling, Juyongguan, Huangyaguan, Jiayuguan Museums have been completed; and the Great Wall Cultural Museums in Jinshanling, Dajingmen and Chongli are under planning, it is a tough and unavoidable task for the construction of Great Wall cultural scenic spot in Baoding, a latecomer, to make innovations in resource integration, function orientation, main products, cultural and museum venues, tourism routes, derivative cultural and creative industries and expression forms.

Fifth, the relationship between the Great Wall in Baoding section and its environment.

It not only refers to the relationship between the Great Wall itself and the natural ecology where it is located, but also refers to the relationship between the Great Wall and the surrounding residential communities, industrial communities and infrastructure.

The folk culture, cultural customs, architectural forms carried by historical villages along the Great Wall are an important part of the cultural ecosystem of the Great Wall, and important resources for the development of cultural tourism products of the Great Wall. They are an inseparable bond of the historical context of the Great Wall, the unforgettable nostalgia for the descendants of the Great Wall guards who traveled far away, and the carrier and medium for visitors to experience the local customs.

Therefore, protecting and inheriting the excellent natural and humane ecological environment around the Great Wall of Baoding is also an important mission for the scientific construction of the Great Wall Cultural Park, which embodies the characteristics, personality and advantages of the Baoding Great Wall Cultural Park.

见证峥嵘岁月　守望幸福生活

周亚梅　刘称心　吴战平

“紫荆关雄视天下，傲立千年，饱经人间冷暖，阅尽聚合离散。壁立如戟曾浸血，荆棘似箭穿史简。招我忠魂伏四夷，兴国赖此忠义胆。”这是易县文联主席李文通先生主编的《雄奇紫荆关》一书开篇的一段话。短短几十字，道尽了紫荆关的前世今生。

作为“内三关”之一，紫荆关长城在历史上的地位举足轻重。往事越千年，古老长城的容颜不断发生着改变，而沉淀在其中的长城精神却历久弥新。

“《雄奇紫荆关》一书是对紫荆关文化的一次梳理总结，也是对长城精神的一次重新认识。早在2011年，易县就提出建设生态文化旅游名城，围绕丰富旅游业态、改善环境、深挖文化等方面做文章。2015年，易县又在河北省率先提出‘全域旅游’的概念，打造清西陵、狼牙山、易水湖等多个景点、景区。在这种背景下，紫荆关镇领导找到我，想让我们出一本关于紫荆关文化的书。我们从2016年底着手，经过大约两年时间，2018年下半年出版了《雄奇紫荆关》一书。”李文通说。

李文通说，在《雄奇紫荆关》搜集、采写、整理、出版的过程中，有不少新发现。如在采写《五勇士夜跳高家片》一文过程中，采写者找到了当时龙华县政府为五勇士颁发的奖状，上面还有时任县长赵鹏飞（后曾任北京市委书记，北京市第八、第九届人大常委会主任）的签名；采写中还挖掘出一家三代人50年守护日军侵华实物证据“津田 ”石碑的故事，并促成把石碑捐献给易县博物馆；等等。这些文物、史料对于研究、展示紫荆关文化有着重要意义。“这对紫荆关文化是一次抢救性的整理和集中展示。”李文通说。

编辑整理《雄奇紫荆关》一书，让李文通对紫荆关文化及紫荆关长城精神有了更深入的认识。他说，山地苦寒，号角连天。在这种边塞文化背景下，历史上的紫荆关人家有兵器，尚武尚兵。他们生性淳朴耿直，崇敬英雄，抵御外侮，誓死不屈，对认定的事或理，有着执着的追求。

“每有烽烟起，战旗此地红。”抗日战争时期，张文海不顾妻子、弟弟等一家11人都被日军抓走严刑拷打的现实，依然坚持斗争； 为了保住党的文件资料，宁死不当俘虏，康翰文、李君玉将文件资料烧毁、藏匿后，把最后一颗子弹留给自己。为了纪念英雄，这才有了后来的文海村、君玉村。

“渐霜风凄紧，关河冷落，残照当楼。”冬日午后，漫步紫荆关长城，城墙上“河山带砺”“紫荆关”的石刻大字依稀。这些跨越了千年的历史沉积在人们的心上，有时厚重得让人想抛也抛不开，因为长城精神已然融入这一方百姓的血脉之中。

“石勒长驱铁骑过，刘琨曾此枕兵戈。”久远的历史不说也罢。且说2012年7月21日的一场暴雨，使紫荆关镇遭遇了1963年以

紫荆关长城

来破坏性最大、损失最为惨重的洪涝灾害，全镇25个行政村全部受灾，交通、电力、通信全部中断，受灾人口逾2万人，直接经济损失高达9.5亿元。

危急关头，全镇人民众志成城、抗灾救灾，创造了“没有一名群众因灾死亡、没有一名游客因洪水滞留”的奇迹，创造了400多天圆满完成恢复重建任务的奇迹。

在脱贫攻坚的主战场，紫荆关群众也不甘落后，大胆摸索，选准项目，敢闯敢试。2002年，紫荆关镇恩村村民汤文民停了跑出租车的营生，在当地率先种植香菇，开一时风气之先。当时谁也想不到，汤文民引领了一个产业的崛起，从此一发而不可收。

紫荆关长城
脚下的村庄

2009年他牵头成立了易县锦兴食用菌农民专业合作社，次年又成立了易县鑫凯食用菌种植有限公司。依托河北师范大学、河北农业大学的技术支持，他不断尝试引进羊肚菌、松茸、灵芝等新品种，拓展市场，助力做大做强食用菌产业。在他的帮助和带动下，附近200多户村民脱贫致富，每户平均年增加收入2万—5万元。

“紫荆关因长城而得名，长城文化、长城精神影响着一代又一代紫荆关人。我们将在团结统一、自强不息、开放包容的长城精神鼓舞下，不断带领干部群众创造更加幸福美好的生活。”紫荆关镇镇长张建军如是说。

Looking Back on the Extraordinary Past and Cherishing the Better-off Present Life

Zhou Yamei Liu Chenxin Wu Zhanping

"Having been overlooking the world for a thousand years, the imposing Zijingguan(Zijing Pass)has experienced the bitter coldness and the spring warmness, and witnessed happy gatherings and sad farewells. Its halberd-like walls were once immersed in blood, and its arrow-like thorns pierced the history book. Staunch countrymen were gathered here to defeat surrounding ethic groups, and the country's revival depended on their loyalty and integrity." Though quite short, the opening paragraph in *The Grand and Imposing Zijingguan*, a book under general editorship of Li Wentong, Chairman of the Literary Federation in Yixian County, depicts well the past and the present of Zijingguan.

Being one of the "Three Inner Passes", Zijingguan has played a prominent part in history. Over time its appearance has been changing, but the spirit of the Great Wall remains timeless.

"Aiming to sort out and summarize Zijingguan culture, the book *The Grand and Imposing Zijingguan* helps us to rediscover the spirit of the Great Wall. Yixian County proposed the idea of building itself into an eco-culture-oriented tourism city as early as in 2011, and has been making efforts to diversify tourism types, improve environment, and delve into culture. In 2015, Yixian County proposed the concept of all-for-one tourism, the first in Hebei Province, and built a number of scenic areas including Western Qing

Tombs, Langya Mountain, and Yishui Lake. It was in such a context that the government officials of Zijingguan Town contacted me to publish a book on Zijingguan culture. We began the work from the end of 2016, and published the book at the second half of 2018." said Li Wentong.

There were quite a few discoveries during the nearly two years' work of collecting data, writing, interviewing, sorting out, and publication of the book, said Li Wentong. In preparing the article "Five Gallant Men Jumping Off the Gaojiapian Cliff at Night", Li and his team found the certificate of merit issued by the then government of Longhua County for the five gallant men, which bore the signature of Zhao Pengfei, the then County Head(he later served as CPC Beijing Municipal Committee Secretary, and the Director of the 8th and 9th NPC Standing Committee of Beijing). During an interview, Li learned that three generations of a family, over 50 years, had been guarding a "Jintian" stone tablet, an evidence of the Japanese invasion into China, and managed to donate the stone tablet to the Museum of Yixian County. These historical stories and relics are of great importance in studying and revealing Zijingguan culture. "We dug up the almost forgotten past events, and unveiled Zijingguan culture in a centralized manner," Li Wentong continued.

In preparing the book *The Grand and Imposing Zijingguan*, Li Wentong understood better the culture and spirit embodied by Zijingguan. The mountainous area was bitterly cold; war horns could be heard far. Living in a frontier fortress region made the people here who possessed weapons admired soldiers and force. Simple and upright, they revered heroes and heroines, defended foreign aggression and wouldn't yield in exchange for life. They had a striking perseverance in upholding their faith.

"Whenever beacon fire was seen, war flags would redden the place." During the anti-Japanese war, Zhang Wenhai didn't surrender even after knowing all his family, 11 members including his wife and younger brother, were taken away and tortured by Japanese troops. Kang Hanwen and Li Junyu, to save the Party's files, refused to be captives at the cost of life — they burned and hid the files and used the last bullets on themselves. Two villages were named after them: Wenhai Village and Junyu Village.

"The frosty wind feels even chillier, making the great river and mountains bleak and desolate, and the setting sun glows on the buildings." In a winter afternoon, along Zijinguan, the stone inscriptions on the Great Wall — "He shan Dai li"(meaning one's resolution will not be even the slightest shaken over time)and the name "Zijingguan" can be faintly seen. A thousand years of history and the spirit of the Great Wall have been in the blood of people here, too overwhelming to be forgotten sometimes.

"Emperor Shi Le of Later Zhao and his cavalry marched to the place; General Liu Kun led the army against him." The remote history is long gone and let's say something more recent. In July 21st, 2012, a rainstorm inflicted a flood calamity on Zijingguan Town, the most devastating and costly one since 1963. All the 25 villages under the town were hit, traffic, power, and communications all disrupted. Over 20,000 people were affected and direct economic loss amounted to RMB 950 million.

People in the town united to fight against the disaster and created literally a miracle: in the end the disaster killed no one and not a single tourist was stranded; reconstruction was finished in just over 400 days.

Nor do Zijingguan people lag behind in poverty alleviation. Bold and courageous, they know how to choose suitable projects. In 2002, Tang Wenmin, a villager in En Village of Zijingguan Town, stopped making a living as a taxi driver and ventured to plant mushrooms, the first in the place. It had never occurred to him or anyone else that he ushered in the rise of an industry. His business keeps thriving. In 2009 he took the lead to establish Jinxing Farmers' Specialized Cooperative of Edible Mushrooms and founded Yixian County Xinkai Edible Mushroom Planting Company the next year. With technical support from Hebei Normal University and Hebei Agricultural University, he made frequent attempts to introduce new species including morchella esculenta, tricholoma matsutake, and lucid ganoderma, so as to expand the market and boost the edible mushroom industry. With his help, over 200 households of villagers nearby have been lifted out of poverty and become better off, with average annual income up by RMB 20,000-50,000 each.

"This place got its name from the Zijingguan Great Wall, and its culture and spirit have been influencing our people one after another generation.

Motivated by such a spirit characterized by unity, resilience, openness, and inclusiveness, we will lead the government cadres and people to create a better life." said Zhang Jianjun, Mayor of Zijingguan Town.

紫荆关长城

紫荆关里那老树

李岩　曹云鹏

走在沉浸于冬日暖阳的紫荆关，寒风从耳边嗖嗖而过，仍忍不住把整张脸露出来深呼吸，享受一下凛冽的清爽。蹚在高过小腿的荒草中，时时发出积雪被踩踏的咯吱声和干枝被踩断的咔吧声。

“十月的雪赛过铁。”易县紫荆关镇白家庄村党支部副书记郭宝群边走边说，“我们这里10月就算入冬了，一旦下雪就得等到来年春天才能化。”他停下来指着不远处：“就是那棵树。”

顺着郭宝群指的方向望去，空旷的天地间，一棵古杨树突兀耸立，它神秘而安静，似一位老人眺望着紫荆关，眺望着依山而延的古长城。古杨树龄300年，树围约8米，高约30米，2016年被纳入古树名木保护名录。

在这寒冷的季节，它虽已卸去盛夏时的满树繁华，但在晴空映衬之下，那纵横交错、屈曲盘旋的虬枝更加清晰，尽显苍劲之美。轻抚树干，那一道道干裂、深邃的树纹如老者手掌间的褶皱，写满岁月的痕迹，倾诉着历史沧桑和流年变迁。牢牢扒于地面的裸根遒劲有力，根内似有源源不断的能量涌动，输送养分到树身，直至每个枝丫末梢，让人感叹生命的顽强。

“我们小时候，这树就像现在这么粗，六个人手拉手才能合围起来。孩子们经常三五成群地在古树下玩耍，听老人们讲那些有关长城和古树的故事……”郭宝群在树下回忆着儿时的美好，“一次意外，这树干被火烧了一个大洞，人们都以为这树活不成了，没想到它竟自然愈合了，现在被烧的痕迹已看不出来了。”

说起这棵古杨的由来，相传宋朝，辽兵屡犯中原，一次从现在的张家口进犯涞源，当时镇守紫荆关的杨六郎奉命迎敌。扎营白家庄时，杨六郎将一棵杨树苗栽于营盘一侧，意为“要把杨家这面保家卫国的大旗竖起来，让辽兵不敢进犯中原”。此后这棵杨树在白家庄村民的管护下茁壮成长，就像杨家“精忠报国”的精神一样历经千年风雨而不衰。虽然这只是一个传说，但反映出紫荆关人的家国情怀和深入骨髓的坚韧、勇敢精神。

古老的传说和顽强的生命力给古树增添了几分神秘。古杨不仅彰显着兴盛与活力，还寄托了白家庄村民对美好生活的向往，被喻为庇护全村的“神树”。也许是巧合，白家庄村是当地有名的长寿村，目前村内90岁以上的老人有18名，他们大多身体结实，还能下地干活儿。白家庄还是十里八乡有名的文化村，每年都有考上大学的孩子从这里走向全国各地，前前后后有60多名大学生。

“随着古杨的知名度越来越大，不少外地人慕名而来，看看这棵传说中杨六郎栽下的古树，量一量它到底有多粗。它都成我们村的旅游‘名片’了。”郭宝群说。

紫荆关内，像白家庄古杨这样的古树还有不少，如南城司乡建国村高18米的古槐、上陈驿村的古黄连树、白家庄的联姻

紫荆关的老杨树

紫荆关的老杨树

树……不少古树背后都有美丽的传说。据《雄奇紫荆关》一书记载，紫荆关区域为我国第一阶梯向第二阶梯的过渡带，区域内海拔高差1600多米。拒马河从玉山铺入境，流经该区域32.5公里。这里年平均气温在10 ℃以下，低于全县水平，年平均降水量650毫米，高于全县平均水平约15%。多样的地貌、独特的气候、充沛的水量，造就了这里品类丰富的植物。目前，区域内由林业和园林部门登记在册的古树名木43株，其中树龄500年以上的一级古树名木8株。

其实，紫荆关林木资源丰富自古有之。《易县志》载，金朝以前，易县有大量的原始森林。金朝诗人蔡松年曾赞叹“春风北卷燕赵，无处不桑麻”。易县紫荆关、五回岭等地皆有茂密的森林。到元明时期，因建都北京，加速了对易县原始森林的破坏。清朝以来，由于农业生产进一步发展，人口增加，加上旗地扩充，加快了易县垦荒的速度。从清顺治元年至乾隆十年（1644—1745），开荒共1.1万亩。到1949年，全县仅存原始次生林2.13万亩，主要分布在蔡家峪的摩天岭、良岗的五回岭、紫荆关及西陵的云蒙山一带，人工林为5892亩，森林覆盖率为0.7%。

新中国成立后，易县大力推动植树造林、荒山育林、林木管理工作。1957年，全县林地面积5.3万亩；1988年，林地面积103.5万亩，森林覆盖率为27.2%；2019年，完成人工造林6.5万亩，封山育林6万亩，森林覆盖率达到56.3%。经过几代人的努力，易县的生态修复和建设发生了翻天覆地的变化。

岁月静淌，古树枝繁叶茂，新木茁壮成长，它们伫立在长城之边，见证着历史，诉说着未来。

The Old Tree in Zijingguan

Li Yan Cao Yunpeng

Wandering at Zijingguan shrouded by winter sunshine, cold wind swished beside ears. I could not help exposing my face to take a deep breath and enjoy the brisk, refreshing air. As we waded calf-deep through weeds, snow squished and dry twigs cracked.

"Snow of October is harder than iron," said Guo Baoqun, Deputy Secretary of the Party Branch of Baijiazhuang Village of Zijingguan Town, Yixian County, as he walked. "Winter begins in October here. Once it snows, the snow does not melt until the next spring." He stopped and pointed at a tree not far away, "That's the tree."

I saw an ancient poplar standing aloft in an open field. It is mysterious and quiet as if an old man was overlooking Zijingguan and the ancient Great Wall extending along the mountains. The poplar is 300 years old, about 8 meters thick and 30 meters tall. The tree was included in the protection list of ancient trees and famous trees in 2016.

Although the tree has shaken off its green ornaments in this cold season, the crisscrossed and winding branches and twigs seem more distinctly vigorous against the background of a clear sky. Gentling touching its truck, you would get a feeling that these cracked, profound bark grains are just like the wrinkles on the hand of an old man — they are traces of the elapsed time telling a story about the vicissitudes of history and changes of time. The bare roots of the tree firmly grasp the soil underneath, in which it seems there are endless energy surging, as well as nutrients transported to its body and even to the end of every twig, provoking an awe of the tenacity of life.

"When we were little kids, the tree was as thick as it is now. Six people joined hands to encircle it. Kids often played in groups under the tree, and listened to the old stories about the Great Wall and the ancient tree..." Guo Baoqun recalled his childhood of happiness under the tree, "In one accident, the trunk was burned to a big hole. And people thought the tree could not survive. To our surprise, it healed naturally. Now, you cannot see any trace of burn."

The origin of this ancient poplar goes back to a legend in the Song dynasty. At that time, the Liao troops invaded repeatedly the Central Plain. In one of these missions, Liao troops invaded Laiyuan from what is now Zhangjiakou, to be met by Yang Liulang(the sixth son of the Yang Warrior Family)who at the time was garrisoned at Zijingguan. After camping at the Baijiazhuang Village, Yang Liulang planted a poplar seedling alongside his barracks to symbolize that "the Yang family was determined to lift up the banner of protecting the nation and resisting the Liao troops outside of the Central Plain". Since then, the poplar had been growing sturdily under the care of Baijiazhuang villagers, just like the ever-lasting "loyal and patriotic spirit" of the Yang Family. Despite being a legend, the story indeed reflects the persistent homeland attachment and the fortitude and courage deep down in the marrow of people living around Zijingguan.

The ancient legend and tenacious vitality add a bit of mystery to the ancient tree. The ancient poplar not only displays prosperity and vitality, but also embodies the villagers' yearning for a better life. It is considered as a "sacred tree" protecting the whole village. Maybe it's a coincidence that Baijiazhuang is known for its longevity. There are now 18 people over the age of 90, most of whom are healthy and able to work in the farmland. Baijiazhuang is also a famous cultural village. Every year many students from here are admitted to universities all over the country. Over the years, there have been altogether more than 60 college students from this village. "As the popularity of the ancient poplar grows, it has attracted many tourists, who travel here to take a look at the ancient tree planted by the legendary Yang family and measure how thick it is. It has become our village's 'tourism card'." Guo Baoqun says.

In Zijingguan, there are many ancient trees like the ancient poplar of Baijiazhuang Village, including the 18-meter-tall locust tree in Jianguo Village of the Nanchengsi Town, the ancient coptis chinensis tree in Shangchenyi Village, and the marriage tree in Baijiazhuang Village... Many ancient trees have beautiful legends. According to the book *the Grand Zijingguan*, the Zijingguan area is the transition zone from the first step to the second step in China's topography, with an altitude difference of more than 1,600 meters. Juma River enters from Yushanpu and flows through this area for 32.5 kilometers. The annual average temperature is below 10 degrees Celsius, which is lower than the average level of the county, and the annual average precipitation is 650 millimeters, which is about 15% higher than average level of the county. The diverse landform, unique climate and abundant water contribute to the rich variety of plants here. At present, there are 43 ancient and famous trees registered by the Forestry and Landscape Department in this region, including 8 first-class ancient and famous trees that are over 500 years old.

In fact, Zijingguan has rich forest resources since ancient times. As recorded in *Yixian Chronicles*, before the Jin Dynasty, Yixian County had a large number of primeval forests. Cai Songnian, a poet of Jin Dynasty, once praised that "the spring breeze sweeps across the land of Yan-Zhao, and there are mulberry and hemp everywhere". Zijingguan, Wuhuiling and other places in Yixian County have dense forests. In the Yuan and Ming Dynasties, the destruction of the primeval forests in Yixian County was accelerated due to the establishment of Beijing as the capital. Since the Qing Dynasty, further development of agricultural production, the increase of population and the expansion of bannerman's land accelerated the reclamation of wasteland in Yixian County. From the first year of Shunzhi to the tenth year of Qianlong in the Qing Dynasty(1644-1745), 11,000 mu(one mu refers to a Chinese unit of land measurement that is commonly 666.7 square metres)of wasteland was reclaimed. By 1949, there were only 21,300 mu of primeval secondary forest in the county, mainly distributed in Motian Ridge in Caijiayu, Wuhui Ridge and Zijingguan in Lianggang, and Yunmeng Mountain in Xiling. There were 5,892 mu of artificial forests, with a forest coverage rate of 0.7%.

After the foundation of the People's Republic of China, Yixian County vigorously promoted tree planting, barren hill afforestation and forest management. In 1957, the county's forestland area was 53,000 mu; in 1988, it was 1.035 million mu, with the forest coverage rate of 27.2%; in 2019, the artificial afforestation area was 65,000 mu, the forest conservation area was 60,000 mu, and the green area ratio reached 56.3%. Through the efforts of several generations, the ecological restoration and construction of Yixian County has undergone great changes.

As time flies, the branches and leaves of ancient trees have become luxuriant, and the new woods are thriving. They stand on the edge of the Great Wall, witnessing the history and telling the story of future.

故国中山　长城归来

苏兰生　苑永涛　罗大庆

这是中国长城的“长寿之星”，已静卧保定西部、北部的山巅2300多年，但直到1988年，才被确认真实存在。

不过，言其“有”的证词早就在民间。

春日里，记者一行到唐县水头村，村里多位年过60岁的村民说，在50年前他们就知道这道古墙，并且是亲眼所见。

村民安德康就是其中的一位。他说，20世纪70年代，他在村北的马耳山砍柴时看到，山峰西侧的鞑子崖附近就有一段齐腰高的石头墙。马耳山是唐县、顺平县交界处的一座高山，因马耳朵似的两座山峰高耸云端而得名。鞑子崖是悬崖绝壁，如天工削切而成，难以攀缘，可崖壁的上面却是一块宽阔的平地。平地的石灰岩中，还凿有一个舂米用的石臼。

不过，这道石墙何时所建，用途为何，时至如今，多数村民仍说不清楚，在惊奇之外也生发不少猜测。

这也难怪，因为直到1988年考古工作者才在唐县的唐河东岸，发现这道石砌长城遗迹，从此湮没太久的中山长城告白世人。安德康说：“上小学时，读过《东郭先生和狼》的课文，是中山国的故事。现在才知道，这个故事的发生地，离咱们这么近呀！”这位对历史不甚了了的村民，当听说村北山上的是中山长城时，对双脚就站在古代的中山国发出如此感叹。

可中山又是怎样的一个国呢？

这是东周时期陕北及晋西北一代的游牧民族白狄鲜虞部，在晋悼公（前586—前558）时，迫于秦国压迫，同时受晋国“和戎政策”的诱惑，南下、东进至太行山东麓建立的一个神秘诸侯国。

史载，鲜虞最早见于公元前774年，分白狄和赤狄。公元前506年，白狄鲜虞在有险可守的中人城（今唐县西北栗山）建国，因城中有山改称“中山”，中山之名开始见于史书。此后，史书

战国中山长城唐县万里段

中兼称鲜虞、中山。至战国时期，这个诸侯国已属于“千乘之国”，成为仅次于七国的二等强国，国君被周王册封为侯。

悠悠历史悠悠水。中山国主要活动区域是今石家庄中北部和保定南部的太行山东麓，这片水土养成中山国民奋进、自立、顽强的性格。中山国在存续200多年的峥嵘岁月中，演绎了几度灭国、几度复国的历史传奇。

中山国曾多次与晋国交战。公元前505—前504年，晋国两次专心进攻鲜虞中山国。公元前414年，中山武公初立，定都于顾（今定州市，一说晋州市），收复失地并开辟了新疆域。公元前406年，中山国为魏国所灭，但不绝嗣。公元前380年左右，中山国又复国。按《中国长城》一书记载，公元前378年，中山国迁都于灵寿古城。

此后，赵国将中山国视为心腹之患。从公元前307年开始，赵武灵王率军连年向中山国进攻。赵惠文王三年（前296），历经七代国君的中山国终为赵国所灭，成为赵国的中山郡。

200多年中山，至此了结。而中山长城却未终结，“中山之问”也在待解。

《史记·赵世家》记载，赵成侯六年（前369），中山筑长城。翻阅资料，这道长城起讫地点，多是记载笼统或缺少实证。最早建国之地，有唐县、古灵寿、正定等不同说法。迁都古灵寿之时，也所记不同。凡此种种，给了人们一张难以应答的历史考卷。

究其走向，这道长城实是拐弯抹角，其北起涞源县，进唐县，过顺平县，再转入唐县，最后进入曲阳县，在蜿蜒山巅和沟谷之间拐来拐去，现在测量的总长度约89公里。长城的结构分石砌和土石混砌两种，和后来的长城一样，也有烽燧和屯军之城，烽燧在险要处，关口筑城，墙内侧修筑屯戍点。

《河北省志·长城志》记载，中山长城城址有20处，烽燧、屯戍点等遗迹有4处。

最北的城址在涞源县黄土岭村东北，应为中山国前沿隘口。城址处在两山沟谷中，长约450米，宽约200米。墙体为石砌，两侧块石略经打制，内填碎石、褐土，底宽约3.5米，残高0.8—3米。城址内，有少量战国夹砂灰陶绳纹陶片、明朝青花瓷片等。据称，此段中山长城明朝曾修缮利用。

最西的曲阳县党城城址处在丘陵地带，面积约37万平方米，现存东、南和西南三段城墙，当地人称“月牙城”。《史记·赵世家》记载：“（赵武灵王）二十一年……合军曲阳，攻取丹丘、华阳、鸱之塞。”丹丘在曲阳县西北，海拔1870米的大茂山为古之恒山，党城正处于恒山之阳。“丹丘”“党”音韵相近，“党”或许就是“丹丘”的谐音，党城可能是中山国的丹丘故城。

至今，这道古墙已年至2300多岁，成为河北境内最早的长城。顺平县文物保管所所长陈建忠说，中山长城比秦始皇修筑的长城大约还早200年。因为距今太为久远，中山长城的墙体坍塌已不成墙状，当地人都形象地称之“土龙”或“龙脊”。尽管如此，穿越2000多年的所有古都城，至今已湮没难觅，而中山长城仍旧傲世临风。

历史钩沉，中山归来。神秘的中山国历经重重磨难，被强国占领又复生，受列国包围而壮大，为大国所欺再变强，不仅创造的经济、文化之辉煌令人刮目相看，而且给保定大地注入了新的

中山长城与明朝长城交接处

精神火种。

中山长城一线，燕、赵和中山等国屡屡用兵，自不待言。仅在日军侵华大“扫荡”中，八路军骑兵团惨烈的“马耳山血战”，已留作人们世代相传的永久记忆。陈建忠计划拍摄一部《长城脚下是我家》的专题片，让历史与现实、物与人相映衬，将长城性格和人文精神暗含其中。

今天，水头村村外的马耳山脚下建起了一座大规模、现代化食用菌深加工工厂，一条条高等级村路、高速公路与中山长城并行远去。村庄的变迁、村民们图变的追求，给这道久久沉默的边

战国中山长城
唐县风山庄段

墙增添了生气。安德康说：“虽然长城一直就在这里，但现在我们才体会到它的存在。”

（历史文化顾问：河北大学博物馆副馆长、教授李文龙）

Great Revitalization of Zhongshan Culture along the Great Wall

Su Lansheng Yuan Yongtao Luo Daqing

The "longevity star" of the Great Wall of China, nestling among the peaks in the northern and western Baoding for more than 2,300 years, was not confirmed to exist until 1988.

However, the testimony of its existence has been among the folks for a long time.

On a spring day, the journalists went to Shuitou Village of Tang County. Many over-60-year-old villagers said that they knew about this ancient wall 50 years ago and had seen it with their own eyes.

The villager An Dekang was one of them. In the 1970s, he saw a waist-high stone wall near the Dazi Cliff on the west side of the mountain when he was chopping wood on Mount Ma'er on the north of his village. Mount Ma'er is a high mountain at the junction of Tang County and Shunping County, with two peaks like horse ears towering in clouds. Dazi Cliff is an unmountable bold cliff. At the top of the cliff is a flat ground. In the limestone of the flat ground was made a stone mortar for pounding rice.

However, most villagers still don't know when and why the stone wall was built, and there is a lot of speculation beyond surprise.

It was not until 1988 that archaeologists found the relics of the stone-made Great Wall on the east bank of Tang River in Tangxian County. An Dekang said, "When I was in primary school, I read the text '*Mr. Dongguo and the Wolf*', which is the story about the Zhongshan State. Now I am aware that the place where this story took place is so close to us." This villager, who knew little about history, sighed when standing where the ancient Zhongshan State was located, after he heard that the Zhongshan Great Wall is on the north mountain of the village.

And what kind of state was Zhongshan?

It was a mysterious vassal state established by Xianyu Baidi, a nomadic tribe in northern Shaanxi and northwestern Shandong. During the reign of Jin Daogong(586 BC-558 BC), under the oppression of Qin State and the temptation of Jin State's "He-Rong Policy"(Policy of making peace with Rong), they moved south and east to the eastern foot of Taihang Mountain and established the vassal state of Zhongshan.

According to the historical records, the Xian Yu group first appeared in 774 BC, which was divided into Baidi and Chidi. In 506 BC, Xian Yu founded the state in the strategically located city of Zhongren(now Mount Su in the northwest of Tangxian County). Later the city was renamed as Zhongshan because there were mountains in the city. The name of Zhongshan began to appear in historical records. Since then, it has been called Xianyu and Zhongshan in history books. By the Warring States Period, this vassal state had become "a state with a thousand chariots", a power only second to the seven stronger states, and its leader was ennobled with the title of duke by the King of Zhou.

The history was a long and winding river. The main area of the Zhongshan State was the eastern foot of Taihang Mountain in the north-central part of Shijiazhuang and the southern part of Baoding. The water and soil here has cultivated the national character of endeavor, independence and tenacity. During the eventful times of its existence for over 200 years, it has performed a historical legend of the destruction and restoration of the country several times.

Zhongshan State fought wars with Jin State many times. From 505 BC to 504 BC, Jin State devoted itself to attacking Zhongshan City of Xianyu. In 414 BC, Wugong, the king of Zhongshan State, established his capital at Gu(today's Dingzhou, or Jinzhou), and recovered the lost territory and opened up a new territory. In 406 BC, the State of Zhongshan was destroyed by Wei State, but it was never sacrificed. Around 380 BC, the state was restored.

According to *The Great Wall of China*, in 378 BC, the state moved its capital to the ancient city of Lingshou. Later, Zhao State regarded Zhongshan State as a major threat. Since the beginning of 307 BC, King Wuling of Zhao led his army to attack Zhongshan State repeatedly. In the third year of the reign of King Huiwen(296 BC), Zhongshan State, which had been occupied by seven sovereigns, was finally annihilated by Zhao State, and became Zhongshan County of Zhao.

Zhongshan State, with the history of 200 years, so far ended. However, the Zhongshan Great Wall has not ended, and "the questions on Zhongshan" are still to be solved.

As recorded in the *Records of the Grand Historian:History of Zhao Aristocratic Family*, the Great Wall was built in the sixth year of Zhao Chenghou(369 BC). Looking through the historical documents, the starting and ending places of the Great Wall are mostly recorded in general or lack of empirical evidence. As for the earliest place to build the kingdom, there are different terms including Tangxian County, Ancient Lingshou and Zhengding. All of these give people a history exam which is difficult to answer.

Upon its direction, the Great Wall starts from Laiyuan County in the north, enters Tangxian County, passes through Shunping County, then turns into Tangxian County, and finally enters Quyang County. It turns back and forth between the winding peaks and valleys. Now its total measured length is about 89 kilometers. The structure of the Great Wall is divided into stone and earth-stone mixture. Like the later Great Wall, there are also beacon towers and military garrison walls. Beacon towers are built at critical points, cities at gateways and garrison points inside the walls.

As recorded in *Hebei Province Annals: The Great Wall Volume*, there are 20 sites of Zhongshan Great Wall and 4 sites of garrison and beacon towers.

The northernmost city site is in the northeast of Huangtuling Village in Laiyuan County, and it should be the front pass of Zhongshan State. The site is in the valley of two mountains, about 450 meters long and 200 meters wide. The wall is built of stone. The block stones on both sides are filled with gravel and brown earth. In the site, its bottom width is about 3.5 meters and its residual height is 0.8 to 3 meters. In the city site, there are a small amount of corded pottery pieces of Warring States gray pottery, and blue and white porcelain pieces of the Ming Dynasty. It is said that this part of the Great Wall had been repaired and used in the Ming Dynasty.

The westernmost Dang City of Quyang County is located in the hilly area, covering an area of about 370,000 square meters. There are three sections of city walls in the east, south and southwest. It is known locally as "Crescent City". As recorded in *Records of the Grand Historian:History of Zhao Aristocratic Family*, "In the 21st year of King Wuling, Zhao State massed troops in Quyang County, and took Danqiu, Huangyang and the Fort of Strigidae. There was a Danqiu City in Quyang County. Some called it Danqiu, another name of Hengshan Mountain. The city got its name because it was at the foot of the mountain." Danqiu is in the northwest of Quyang County. Damao Mountain, with an altitude of 1,870 meters, is Hengshan Mountain of ancient times. Dang City is in the south of Hengshan Mountain. "Danqiu" and "Dang" sound similar in Chinese and "Dang" may be the homophone of "Danqiu", so Dang City might be the ancient Danqiu City of Zhongshan State.

Up to now, this ancient wall has reached the age of over 2,300, making it the earliest Great Wall in Hebei Province. According to Chen Jianzhong, director of Cultural Security Institute of Shunping County, the Zhongshan Great Wall was about 200 years earlier than that built by Qin Shihuang(the first emperor of Qin Dynasty). Because of its long history, the wall has collapsed and is no longer in wall shape. The local people figuratively call it as "earth dragon" or "dragon ridge". Nevertheless, all of ancient cities have disappeared through two millenniums of history, but the Great Wall is still there.

As history continues, Zhongshan culture returns. The mysterious Zhongshan State experienced many hardships, occupied by a power and then revived. It grew stronger under the invasion of other states. Its economic and cultural brilliance is impressive. Moreover, it left an eternal spiritual heritage for Baoding.

At the Zhongshan Great Wall, Yan, Zhao, Zhongshan and other states repeatedly used troops. Only in the Japanese aggression against China, the Eighth Route Army Cavalry impressed the later generations with a tragic "Bloody Battle in Ma'er Mountain". Chen Jianzhong plans to make a feature film entitled *My Home Is at the Foot of The Great Wall.* The film will integrate history and reality, things and people to imply the character and humanistic spirit of the Great Wall.

Today, outside Shuitou Village, a large-scale modern edible fungus deep processing factory has been built at the foot of Ma'er Mountain. More than one high-grade village roads and highways extend to the distance with the Zhongshan Great Wall side by side. The change of the village and the pursuit of the villagers add vitality to this long silent flank wall. An Dekang said, "Although the Great Wall has always been here, we did not appreciate its existence until now."

(The consultant on history and culture: Professor Li Wenlong, deputy curator of Hebei University Museum)

战国中山长城
唐县罗庄段

冀晋锁钥地　两路守雄关

苏兰生　罗大庆

古有“未到五台先看寺”的说法。春日里，驱车前往长城岭，离目的地还很远，就有了到清凉世界的感觉。

爬上长城岭，凉风飕飕。西看山峦，空然寂寥；东望沟谷，村庄邈远。长城岭关口处在河北、山西两省交界处，在明朝是长城的一个重要前沿隘口。

明长城在阜平段延伸，有两个特点：一是分属真保镇的两路——倒马关路和龙泉关路；二是长城出涞源县后，沿太行山脉南下，参差分布在河北、山西两省的交界地带。

有明一朝，阜平段长城处在内地，与外长城、京畿之地相比，战略地位次之。所以，长城防线虽长，实际修筑段并不多，多为险要山险。至清朝以后，统治者对这段长城的修护也不够，致使长城遗存较少。

倒马关路管理的长城起于涞源县狼牙口，至阜平县段庄乡铁岭口。据保定市文物管理所调查，此段长城长约80公里，仅有片段城墙，敌台均为茨字号。

在史书记载里，这段长城有古道口、柴皮岭、落路口、刘岭

近看保存较好的城墙

阜平段明长城

口等隘口。今天，这些地名犹存，隘口已了无痕迹，茨字3号、4号、5号台亦不知何方。在铁岭口东约2公里处有一座空心敌楼，门额上石匾字不可辨，应为茨字6号台。楼内保存石碑一座，为万历四年（1576）春防兵部右侍郎兼都察院右佥都御史汪道昆巡道至此所立。

7号、9号台在山西灵丘境内。阜平县境内黄崖西北约2公里处有一敌楼，可能是茨字10号台。从此台向西，灵丘县境内有11号、12号、13号敌楼。再向北，在阜平县境内又出现14号、15号台，两台之间城墙遗址残高不足1米。14号台楼内有一段保存完好的石碑，为万历二年（1574）所立。

吴王口是倒马关路长城较为险要的一个隘口，今关口建筑荡然无存。在吴王口东北通灵丘县的一条沟谷里有16号台，当地称为“下平台楼”，台楼顶完好，楼东南角有一天井可上台顶。17号台被当地称为“上平台楼”，楼顶垛口踏平，为抗日时期受炮轰所致。

从段庄乡铁岭口开始，沿山脉以下的长城由龙泉关路管辖。

长城岭处在龙泉关西约10公里，阜平县与山西五台县交界处。城墙南北走向，关口居其中，墙两端各有一砖砌敌楼。关口北面城墙保存完整，石砌垛口犹存。南端城墙坍塌，已不成墙貌。关门顶部门楼已毁，仅存顶部塌落的拱形门洞。

由长城岭向南，到龙泉关路所辖最南端的三关子口（今三官），与鹞子崖长城相连，进入石家庄市灵寿县，这段长城防线长约62公里。

龙泉关路所辖长城全线，均在崇山峻岭之中，除长城岭一带有近千米城墙和下庄山上有一小段城墙外，其余地段均以山险为障，未筑城墙，仅设有一些隘口和石砌烽火台。阜平县境内歪头山南侧的山梁上，有几座残塌的敌楼和一座石券顶房屋遗迹。黑崖山至长城岭间，有一些毁坏的石砌烽火台。由龙泉关再向南，可见安门沟原有城墙已被水冲毁，现存长度不足10米。黑林沟北

2.5公里处有一座烽火台，北面较完整，其余三面塌成石堆状。三关子处原有3座敌楼，均已塌毁，现仅存遗迹。

龙泉关城为明正统二年（1437）所建的龙泉下关，是通往山西的重要关口。关城分内、外两道，现在均已塌毁，仅存一关门。关城南北两侧与山顶相连的城墙亦已毁坏。

阜平县城至五台山有78公里，龙泉关是五台山寺庙的东大门。据传，沿此路的阜平县境内，兴盛时期有20多座寺院，至今仍有益寿寺、龙宿庵等。

这段长城留有1927—1928年晋奉军阀大战的遗迹。新中国开国十大元帅中有8位曾涉足这里。新《阜平县志》主编高明乡说，诸多抗击日寇的英勇战斗与红色革命、绿色发展、生态文明在此融合，共同构成一个丰富鲜活的系统教育工程，给后人以奋进不息的精神力量。

在此，还留有秦朝大将修路的条石、杨延昭的挂甲树等民间传说、清朝皇帝朝台的故事，以及龙泉关都司秀昆抗击八国联军的战事……

往事已矣，再看今朝。离龙泉关不远处，一幢幢高楼在山谷中拔地而起，演绎着偏远山村变城镇、村民成市民的喜人变迁。

在长城岭上，遥想一桩桩长城战事，您会有着似乎烽烟燃起、铜炮铁铳、滚木礌石、弓箭矢镞，守城官兵抵御入侵之敌的历史想象。车过龙泉关，向东一路前行，您会看见一处处新变化，在冀晋雄关之下也正演绎着一则则扶贫攻坚、百姓脱贫的暖心故事。

（历史文化顾问：河北大学博物馆副馆长、教授李文龙）

The Vital Area between Ji and Jin
The Majestic Pass Guarded by Two Roads

Su Lansheng Luo Daqing

As an old saying goes, "One sees temples before he reaches Wutai". In spring, if you drive to Changchengling Pass, you may feel cool and refreshing before you reach the destination.

On the Great Wall, it is windy and chilly. On the west side, the mountains are serene and solitary; on the east side, villages in valleys are misty. Changchengling Pass, located at the junction of Hebei and Shanxi provinces, was an important frontier pass of the Ming Great Wall.

The extension of the Ming Great Wall in Fuping has the following features: (1) It was under the jurisdiction to two roads in Zhenbao Town — Daomaguan Road and Longquanguan Road; (2) It is unevenly distributed in the border area of Hebei and Shanxi after it moves out of Laiyuan County and descends south along the Taihang Mountain.

In the Ming Dynasty, the Fuping section of the Great Wall is located in the interior, and its strategic position was less important than the exterior Great Wall and the national capital and its neighborhoods. Therefore, although the Great Wall has a long defense line, not many sections were actually constructed, and most of the Wall are dangerous accesses. After the Qing Dynasty, this section of the Great Wall was not well maintained, resulting in the loss of the Great Wall relics.

The Great Wall section managed by Daomaguan Road starts at Langyakou in Laiyuan County, and ends at Tielingkou of Duanzhuang

Town in Fuping County. According to investigations by the Baoding Cultural Relics Management Office, this section is about 80 kilometers long, with only segments of ramparts, and the watchtowers are all Ci-character marked.

In historical records, this section of the Great Wall has passes such as Gudaokou, Chaipiling, Luolukou, Liulingkou, etc. Today, these names still exist, these passes are unseen, and the Ci-character marked No. 3, 4, and 5 watchtowers disappear. About 2 kilometers east of Tielingkou, there is a hollow watchtower, a stone plaque on the gate forehead having indistinguishable characters, and it should be Ci-character marked No. 6 watchtower. There is a stone stele preserved in the building, which was established by Wang Daokun, who was patrolling the passes here as the right assistant minister of the Spring Defense Department and the censor of Court of Censors in the 4th year of Wanli(1576).

No. 7 and No. 9 watchtowers are located in Lingqiu of Shanxi. There is a watchtower about 2 kilometers northwest of Huangya in Fuping County, which may be Ci-character marked No. 10 watchtower. From this station to the west, there are No.11, No. 12, and No. 13 watchtowers in Lingqiu County. Further north, No. 14 and No. 15 are seen in Fuping County, and the height of the city wall relics is less than 1 meter between the two watchtowers . There is a well-preserved stone stele in the No. 14 watchtower, established in the second year of Wanli(1574).

Wuwangkou is a relatively dangerous pass in the Great Wall on Daomaguan Road, and today no buildings can be found at the pass. In a valley in Tonglingqiu County, northeast of Wuwangkou, No. 16 watchtower lies, which is locally called the "lower platform building", with a completely-preserved roof and a patio to the roof at the southeast corner; No.17 watchtower is locally called the "upper platform building", with a collapsed flat crenel of the roof, which was caused by shelling during the Anti-Japanese Period.

Starting from Tielingkou in Duanzhuang, the Great Wall along the mountain range is governed by Longquanguan Road.

The Great Wall Ridge is located about 10 kilometers west of Longquanguan, at the juncture of Fuping County and Wutai County, Shanxi. The city wall runs north-south, with the pass in it, and there is a brick watchtower at each end of the wall. The city wall to the north of the pass is well-preserved, and the stone crenels still exist. The city wall at the south end has collapsed and shows no wall shape anymore. The gatehouse at the top of the gate has been destroyed, leaving only the arched doorway with a collapsed top.

From Changchengling to the south, the Great Wall in this section crosses Sanguanzikou(now Sanguan), the southernmost part of Longquanguan Road, which connects with the Great Wall in Yaoziya and then enters Lingshou County of Shijiazhuang city.

The section of the Great Wall governed Longquanguan Road is distributed in the high mountains and steep cliffs. Except for the nearly 1,000-meter city wall in Chajianling and a short section of the city wall on Xiazhuang Mountain, no city wall was built in the rest of the sections where high mountains could serve as a barrier. In those sections, only some mountain passes and stone beacon towers were built. On the southern ridge of the Waitou Mountain in Fuping County, there are several relics of dilapidated watchtowers, a stone-topped house, and some damaged stone beacon towers between Heiya Mountain and Changchengling. From Longquanguan to the south, the original city wall in Anmengou Village was ruined by water. The existing length is less than 10 meters. There is a beacon tower of 2.5 kilometers north of Heilingou village. Its north side is relatively complete and the other three sides collapse into stone mounds. The three watchtowers at Sanguanzi have all been destroyed, with only the relics left.

The Lower Longquanguan, built in the second year of the Ming Dynasty(1437), is today's Longquanguan City. It is a crucial strategic pass to Shanxi Province. It consists of inner walls and outer walls, both of which have now collapsed, leaving only one pass gate. The city walls on both sides, which are connected to the top of the mountain, have also been destroyed.

Fuping County is 78 kilometers from Wutai Mountain. Longquanguan is the east gate of the Wutai Mountain Temple. It is said that there were more than 20 temples in Fuping County along this road in the prosperous period. Until now, the Yishou Temple and the Longsu Nunnery still exist.

In the Great Wall of Longquanguan section, there are relics of Jin-Feng War between 1927 and 1928. Eight of the top ten marshals of China once set foot there. Gao Mingxiang, editor-in-chief of the new *Fuping County Chronicles*, said that many battles against the Japanese invaders, together with the red revolution, green development and ecological civilization, formed a rich and vivid systematic education project, giving future generations the spiritual strength to forge ahead.

In the Longquanguan section of the Great Wall, there are several folk legends such as the stripe-shaped stone used for road construction by generals in the Qin Dynasty and the "Guajia Tree" of Yang Yanzhao. There are also stories about three Qing emperors worshiping Buddha in Wutai Mountain, and Si Xiukun, a military officer of Longquanguan, who fought against the Eight-Nation Allied Forces.

The past history is long gone, and let's look at the present. Around Longquanguan, tall buildings rise up in the valley, demonstrating the gratifying changes from remote mountain villages to towns, and villagers to citizens. On the ridge of Changchengling, you can visualize a scene of ancient wars, where soldiers defended the city against invaders with bronze cannons, iron blunderbuss, rolling logs and boulders, bows and arrows. While driving through Longquanguan and heading east, you will see changes everywhere. Under the majestic passes of Hebei and Shanxi, there are heart-warming stories about poverty alleviation spreading among people.

(The consultant on history and culture: Professor Li Wenlong, deputy curator of Hebei University Museum)

车到长城岭　边墟辨旧营

苏兰生　刘亚辉　罗大庆

"燕晋分疆处，雄关控上游……虎护千年树，人披六月裘。"清朝曾任雄州知州的严遂成以这样的场面特写，勾勒了龙泉关所处边墟之地的旧时场景。

从保定出发，沿省道阜忻公路驱车1个多小时，来到长城岭爬"野长城"：一座关楼残破、一段墙体斑驳，冷风中，怆然感到苍凉。

不过，推开历史这扇门，可见这残旧的一楼、一墙之中，历史底蕴是那样的厚重。

明长城东出唐县，在阜平县断断续续延伸100多公里。到了龙泉关，在长城岭上又筑起龙泉上关和龙泉下关这样的一个关口和一座城堡。

新《阜平县志》主编高明乡说，长城岭上的关口是龙泉上关；向东距此约10公里的山下，筑有龙泉下关城堡。旧《阜平县志》记载："城西几十里亦五台孙枝，古长城台基尚存……上边有边城，重山复障，奔电吞云，燕晋出入之冲也。"

《河北省志·长城志》记有，龙泉上关初建于明朝永乐年间，龙泉下关建于明正统二年（1437）。景泰二年（1451）、嘉靖二十五年（1546）分别增筑和改筑关城。清顺治十一年（1654），龙泉关和龙泉城堡由茨沟（今属山西省繁峙县）移驻设参将。

在明朝，阜平段长城处在内地。《畿辅通志》记载，明朝的翁万达在《边防修守事宜疏略》上书时说："……紫荆、宁武、雁门为要。次则居庸、倒马、龙泉……"这说明龙泉关的战略地位，比不得京畿、晋北之地显要。

不过，龙泉上关作为冀晋咽喉要道，又在阜平县段明长城的中间位置，所受重视程度也就有了比较优势。《山西通志》记载，龙泉上关为"通京师大路，銮络西行必取道于此。关门虽归直隶辖，而实为三晋全省东北要害，不止为五台山锁钥"。

在长城岭上，关楼修筑在隘口，一条公路在关口南侧穿过。关口为砖券拱形门洞，宽4.4米，高5米，门洞中间顶部坍塌。关门两侧南北向石砌城墙长942米，墙体北段保存尚好，尚存垛口，南段已毁，不成墙状。长城岭段城墙骑墙而筑敌楼2座、墙台3座，敌楼现仅存条石基础，墙台均已塌毁。关楼西口立有一座石碑，为1956年河北省为保护长城所立。

细看城墙，让人提出多个疑问。长城岭长城石土混砌的墙体内，并不是填有同样的石头。有的整块白如羊脂，有的青中泛红，有的灰里透黑，说明这些石头不是来自一个山体。

再看墙面的石头，许多留有劈凿的纹路。这些有着数百年印迹的石块，仅从相同颜色断定，该是来自一座山。而绕长城两侧踏勘，这样的石头在附近山上并没有，证明来自远山。

长城岭长城

从关口空手爬北侧的长城，很是吃力；修筑时，自然会更费力。敌楼的条状基石，最长的有两三米。而城墙的石头，重的动辄上吨。在山险处筑起这道城墙，不用人海战术是不行的。

人们尚不知，当时筑起这段长城，动用了多少军士和百姓。但可肯定，按当时的开凿技术和运输水平，仅靠周边百姓修筑是不够的。高明乡说，阜平段长城上有些大块青砖就留有烧砖人的住址和名字。

从长城岭向东而下，盘山路弯弯曲曲。至山腰，路旁孤立一座石碑，碑文风蚀难辨，石碑紧邻一座方形的低矮小屋。小屋门扉虚掩，屋内底部是一汪甘洌的泉水，这就是当地有许多传说的“马刨泉”。

再向下，进入三面环山的印钞石村，这是沿阜忻公路通向五台山，阜平县境内最西的小山村。明朝，龙泉关路下辖21个隘口，

长城岭长城
部分墙体

印钞石口是其中一个，弘治十五年（1502）始建。村内，有一座面朝东的益寿寺，寺庙的外墙风蚀残破，院子一个角落里冒着潺潺流水。村民们说，在抗战前，这座古寺庙还具有相当规模。

高明乡说，长城岭既是明朝很多战争的战场，也是抗击八国联军的重要战场。1939年6月，盘踞山西五台县的日军500多人越过长城岭，“蚕食”龙泉关一带，因遭受打击退回。随后，日军纠集阜平县周边的山西、河北共6个县的日伪军6000多人合击抗日军民，烧杀抢掠十几天。

从长城岭而归，沿途看到如今的村庄道路、村貌和百姓生活的巨大变化；而一天的野外踏勘，让人感慨古代和近代军事家的谋略，也感受到揭示长城精神，对动员群众和凝聚力量具有的重大现实意义。

Exploring the Ancient Border Barracks along Changchengling

Su Lansheng Liu Yahui Luo Daqing

"Where Yan and Jin borders lies an impregnable pass holding the upper reaches of the Yellow River... Tigers protecting trees of a thousand years and people wearing fur coats in June." This description was written by Yan Suicheng, who once served as the governor of Xiongzhou in the Qing Dynasty, depicting the scene of the border where Longquanguan was located in the past.

Setting off from Baoding and driving along Fuxin highway for more than an hour, we finally reached Chanchengling(The Great Wall Ridge)and started to climb the "wild Great Wall": a wall segment with a dilapidated watchtower, giving a desolate atmosphere in the cold wind.

However, opening the door of history, you can see how rich the historical profundity is in this dilapidated building and rampart.

The Great Wall of the Ming Dynasty starts from Tangxian County to the east, extending intermittently for more than 100 kilometers in Fuping County, and reaches Longquanguan, where Upper Longquanguan and Lower Longquanguan were built on Changchengling, a pass and a fort respectively.

Gao Mingxiang, editor-in-chief of the new *Fuping County Chronicles*, said that the pass on the Ridge of Changchengling is Upper Longquanguan; about 10 kilometers to the east lies Lower Longquanguan Fortress. The old *Fuping County Chronicles* recorded: "For dozens of miles west of the city, the foundation of the ancient Great Wall still exists... There is a border city, and heavy mountains as obstacles, a gateway to enter and get out of Yan and Jin."

Hebei Province Chronicles: The Great Wall Volume records that Upper Longquanguan was first built in the Yongle period of the Ming Dynasty; the Lower Longquanguan was constructed in the second year of Zhengtong in the Ming Dynasty(1437), the second year of Jingtai(1451)and the 25th year of Jiajing(1546)witnessed reconstruction of the fortress. In the eleventh year of Shunzhi in the Qing Dynasty(1654), Longquanguan and Longquanguan Fortress were stationed by generals appointed by Cigou(now in Fanzhi County, Shanxi). Later guerrillas, army and government offices were established in Kangxi and Qianlong periods respectively.

In the Ming Dynasty, the Fuping section of the Great Wall was located inland. *Jifu Tongzhi* records what Weng Wanda of the Ming Dynasty said in his submission *A Brief Description of Border Defense Maintenance*, "Zijing, Ningwu, and Yanmen are the key passes for maintenance, followed by Juyong, Daoma, Longquan...", indicating that the strategic position of Longquanguan is less important than Jingji and northern Jin.

However, Upper Longquanguan, as the key pass of the Ji-Jin(Hebei-Shanxi)path, is in the middle of the Ming Great Wall in Fuping County, so it was given great attention. *Shanxi Chronicles* records that Upper Longquanguan is "the main road to the capital and the must-take road to the west. The pass is under the jurisdiction of Zhili, and it is actually the key access to the northeast of Jin(Shanxi Province), not just the key access to Wutai Mountain".

On the ridge of Changchengling, the main building of the fortress is located at the mountain pass, and a road goes through the pass in the south. The gateway is an arched brick gate with a width of 4.4 meters and a height of 5 meters. The middle top of the gateway has collapsed. The north-south stone wall on both sides of the gate is 942 meters long. The northern part of the wall is well-preserved with crenels on it. The southern part, which has been destroyed, is no longer in good shape. Two watchtowers and three platforms were built along the ramparts of the Changchengling section. A strip-shaped stone foundation is the only remaining section of the watchtower, and all the platforms have collapsed. There is a stone tablet at the west entrance of the building, which is engraved with "the Great Wall of Changchengling", which was erected in 1956 to protect the Great Wall in Hebei Province.

A close look at the city walls could trigger a number of doubts. Firstly, the walls mixed with stone and soil are not filled with the identical stones in the Great Wall of Changchengling. Some are as white as lanolin, some are reddish in green, and some are black in gray. That shows the stones are not from the same mountain.

Second, looking at the stones on the wall, you may find that many of them have chiseled lines. Judging by their identical color, these stones, with marks dating back hundreds of years, are most probably from the same mountain. However, surveying around the Great Wall, you may discover that such stones cannot be found in the nearby mountains, which proves that they are from distant mountains.

It can be strenuous when climbing the northern section of the Great Wall empty-handed from the pass. Apparently, the construction of it is more laborious. The longest strip-shaped cornerstone of the watchtower is two to three meters long, while the stone of the city wall generally weighs tons. It is impossible to build this city wall in a dangerous place without a crowd of laborers.

It is yet not known how many soldiers and civilians were involved in building this section of the Great Wall. However, it is certain that according to the excavation technology and transportation capacity at that time, only the surrounding residents were not sufficient for this construction work. Gao Mingxiang said that on the Great Wall of Fuping, there are some large black bricks made of burnt wood, on which the address and name of each brick maker are inscribed.

From Changchengling to the east, the mountain road twists and turns. On the hillside, there is an isolated stone tablet beside the road, next to a low square hut. The inscriptions on the tablet is hardly distinguishable due to wind erosion. The door of the hut is left open, and there is a sweet spring at the bottom of the house, which is a local spring named "Mapao Spring" in many legends.

Going down the ridge, you may enter the Chaoyinshi Village, which is surrounded by mountains on three sides. This village is the westernmost mountain village along the Fuxin Highway leading to Wutai Mountain and Fuping County. In the Ming Dynasty, Longquanguan Road had

21 subordinate mountain passes, one of which was Chaoyinshi Pass. Its construction work started since the fifteenth year of Hongzhi(1502). In the village, there is the Yishou Temple facing east. The outer wall of the temple is damaged by wind erosion, and there is gurgling water in a corner of the courtyard. Villagers said that before the war, the temple was still quite large.

Gao Mingxiang said that many wars in the Ming Dynasty took place on Changchengling, which was also an important battlefield against the Eight-Nation Allied Forces. Only in June 1939, more than 500 Japanese soldiers stationed in Wutai County of Shanxi Province, crossed Changchengling and "encroached" the Longquanguan area, but retreated due to the attack. Subsequently, the Japanese invaders gathered more than 6,000 Japanese and puppet troops from six counties in Shanxi and Hebei Province around Fuping County for joint attack. Along the way, they burned, killed and looted for more than ten days.

Returning from Changchengling, along the way, we could see the great changes in today's village roads, village appearance and people's residences. While reminiscing over the day's field surveys, we felt amazed at the strategies of ancient and modern military strategists. Additionally, we deeply felt that exploring the spirit of the Great Wall is of great practical significance to mobilize the masses and gather their strength.

龙泉雄关故事多

米冬冬　李娜　贾祎玮　罗大庆

在东距阜平县城35公里、西北距五台山30公里的山巅，矗立着威名赫赫的长城雄关——龙泉关。作为明朝防御关外少数民族入侵所建设的军事设施，龙泉关留下了数代帝王的故事，也见证了清王朝闭关锁国、软弱挨打的历史。

龙泉关有上、下两关，相距5公里。龙泉上关建于明朝永乐年间，龙泉下关始建于明朝正统二年（1437），万历四年（1576）重修，呈南北走向，总长约1公里，中间是关门，两边各有马道、战台、敌楼。现存龙泉关城遗址为砖砌城墙的上关关城，北门向南开，砖拱门洞，宽3.5米，深10米，由大型条石砌基。明清两朝一直有驻兵把守龙泉关，设置在龙泉关南山上的古营盘（军营）遗址至今尚存。

明清时，龙泉关为从北京去往山西的必经之路。明朝诗人释德清在赴五台山时路过龙泉关，见此雄关苍凉曲折，感慨赋诗云："策杖烟霞外，重关虎豹林。路当崎曲险，山入寒垣深。惨淡黄云色，萧条落日阴。边笳如怨客，呜呜岭头吟。"时至今日，在龙泉关一带还流传着清朝皇帝过龙泉关的故事。

龙泉关

旗杆石

新《阜平县志》的主编高明乡对古长城和阜平县历史颇有研究。他为记者讲述了关于清朝皇帝的传说：“清朝康熙帝在去山西巡视的路上，途经龙泉关一带时，在招提寺看见一座峥嵘突兀的山峰迎面矗立，显得特别高大。康熙便吩咐左右：射箭超过山顶的奖银五十两。然而众人所射的箭，到半山腰就飘飘落下。康熙亲自引弓连发三箭，‘皆逾峰巅’，从此这座山就叫‘三箭山’，悬崖中部刻有‘三箭山’三个大字。”清乾隆时期，直隶总督方观承在此立下石碑纪念此事，乾隆皇帝还亲自撰写了碑文。

相比于乾隆皇帝和直隶总督方观承“背书”的“三箭山传说”，另外一则康熙帝微服过龙泉关的传说，则更有乡土气息。相传康熙帝（一说为清光绪帝）微服过龙泉关时，守关士兵令其下驴接受检查。书童道：“这是当今天子。”士兵道：“就是康熙皇帝从此过，也得检查后放行。”康熙非常赞赏士兵的负责精神，便将原本为五品的守将官职提升为四品，同时授予这名士兵进京面君的特权。

清康熙四十一年（1702），皇子胤禛随其父康熙帝去五台山礼佛，路过龙泉关时曾留下了诗作《恭谒五台过龙泉关偶题》：“隔断红尘另一天，慈云常护此山巅。雄关不阻骖鸾客，胜地偏多应迹贤。兵象销时崇佛像，烽烟靖始扬炉烟。治平功效无生力，赢得村翁自在眠。”

龙泉关素为冀晋咽喉要道，地理位置十分重要，自古以来便是兵家必争之地。因此龙泉关周边先后发生过不少战事。

宋朝时，尚未建有龙泉关，便有杨六郎在此与辽国交战的记载。

清朝顺治年间，农民起义军曾攻破龙泉关，攻陷阜平城。

1900年，八国联军攻破北京。1901年1月，八国联军中的德国军队从定州出发，向龙泉关进攻，意欲由此攻入山西。龙泉关都

土芯城墙

司秀昆率部组织乡民，顽强抵抗前来进犯的德军，给予德军一定的打击。但装备落后的清军不是装备精良的德军的对手，德军最终攻破龙泉关。秀昆率残部退往山西境内，最终在五台山苏子坡全军覆没。龙泉关再次被攻破，见证了清朝落后挨打、屡受外辱的历史。

往事已随风而逝，曾经的雄关也已残破不全，但龙泉关所见证的历史，给后人带来无尽的警醒和反思。

Myriad Legends of the Majestic Longquanguan

Mi Dongdong   Li Na   Jia Yiwei   Luo Daqing

On the top of the mountain, 35 kilometers away from Fuping County in the east and 30 kilometers away from Wutai Mountain in the northwest, stands a majestic pass of the Great Wall — Longquanguan. As a military facility built in the Ming Dynasty to defend against the invasion of ethnic minorities outside the pass, Longquanguan left behind stories of several generations of emperors, and witnessed the history of the Qing Dynasty, which became increasingly weak and subjected to foreign invasion due to the closed door policy.

Longquanguan was built in 1437, the second year of Emperor Zhengtong in the Ming Dynasty, and rebuilt in 1576, the fourth year of Emperor Wanli in the Ming Dynasty. Longquanguan is a north-south pass with a total length of about 1 kilometers. In the middle is the gate of the pass with horse tracks, battle platforms and watchtowers on either side. Longquanguan has two passes up and down, five kilometers apart. The existing site of Longquanguan City is Shangguan Pass City with brick walls. The north gate opens to the south. The brick archway is 3.5 meters wide and 10 meters deep, with large strips of stone as its foundation. During the Ming and Qing Dynasties, Longquanguan was always guarded by garrisons. The ancient barracks remains intact on the Nanshan Mountain of Longquanguan.

In the Ming and Qing Dynasties, Longquanguan was the only access from Beijing to Shanxi. De Qing, a poet of the Ming Dynasty, passed Longquanguan when he went to Wutai Mountain. Seeing the desolation and tortuousness of the grand pass, he sighed, and composed a poem, "Carrying a cane in my hand, I walked towards the fortified passes in the mist of clouds under the twilight. In the distance, the ramparts wound its way along the dangerous road in the chilly wind. In the sunset, the clouds were tinted with pale yellow, which created desolate atmosphere. I heard the sound of the Bianjia flute, like a plaintive traveller singing the lament of sorrow on the mountain top." Today, the story of the emperor crossing Longquanguan in the Qing Dynasty still circulates among local residents.

Gao Mingxiang, editor-in-chief of the new *Fuping County Chronicles*, has conducted plenty of research on the ancient Great Wall and the history of Fuping County. He told reporters about two legends of Emperors in the Qing Dynasty, "When Emperor Kangxi passed through Longquanguan on an inspection tour to Shanxi, he found himself standing face-to-face with a towering mountain peak in the Zhaoti temple. Kangxi ordered his followers: "whoever can shoot over the top of the mountain will be rewarded with fifty silver taels." But the arrows that they shot fell halfway up the mountain. Kangxi himself drew a bow and shot three arrows in succession. "All of them went beyond the peak." From then on, this mountain was called "Sanjianshan"(Three Arrow Mountain). In the middle of the cliff were inscribed three big characters: "San-Jian-Shan". During the reign of Emperor Qianlong in the Qing Dynasty, Fang Guancheng, the governor of Zhili, set up a stone tablet here to commemorate the event. Emperor Qianlong also wrote the inscriptions himself. The stone tablet is now preserved on the wall of the Zhaoti temple, and Qianlong's inscriptions are clearly visible.

Compared with the "Sanjianshan Legend" endorsed by Emperor Qianlong and Zhili governor Fang Guancheng, the other legend that Emperor Kangxi went through Longquanguan is more rustic. It is said when Emperor Kangxi(one said to be Emperor Guangxu of the Qing Dynasty), passed through Longquanguan incognito, the garrison soldier ordered him to get off his donkey for inspection. The Servant of the Emperor said, "This is the son of Heaven(Emperor)". The soldier responded, "Even if Emperor

Kangxi himself passed from here, he had to be inspected first and then released." Emperor Kangxi highly appreciated the soldier's strong sense of responsibility, so he promoted the soldier's position from the fifth grade to the fourth grade and granted the soldier the privilege of entering the capital to meet him.

In the 41st year of Emperor Kangxi in the Qing Dynasty(1702), the prince Yinzhen accompanied his father Kangxi to worship Buddha at Wutai Mountain. When passing Longquanguan, he composed a poem named *A Improvised Poem When Passing through Longquanguan on the Way to Yuntai Mountain*: "Cut off from the human vanity for another realm, the mountain is permeated in the mist of clouds. Majestic pass could not hinder the aspiring mind, historical attractions fostered many heroes. Buddha worship pervaded once the signs of war, the ash in incense burner was poured away after the war. My ambition of governing the country and bringing peace to the world has not been achieved, I can sleep here soundly as a villager."

As a strategic junction between Hebei and shanxi, Longquanguan has a crucial geographical location, and it has been the place that has geographic advantage for military strategists since ancient times. Many wars broke out around Longquanguan area.

In the Song Dynasty, when Longquanguan had not yet been built, Yang Liulang(Yang Yanzhao)battled against the Liao army here.

During the reign of Emperor Shunzhi in the Qing Dynasty, the peasant uprising army once conquered Longquanguan and captured Fuping.

In 1900, the Eight-Nation Allied Forces conquered Beijing. In January 1901, the German army of the Eight-Nation Allied Forces set out from Dingzhou and attacked Longquanguan, intending to invade Shanxi from here. Xiu Kun, the military officer of Longquanguan, led his troops together with villagers to resist the invading army and finally gave a blow to the German Army. However, the Qing army, with its weak military system and backward equipment, was not the rival of the well-equipped German army. The invading army eventually broke through Longquanguan. Xiukun led the rest of the army to retreat to Shanxi, and was eventually annihilated in Suzipo in Wutai Mountain. Longquanguan was breached again, witnessing the history of backwardness and humiliation in the Qing Dynasty .

Things have gone with the wind, and the once majestic pass has been dilapidated, but the history witnessed by Longquanguan has brought endless warnings and reflections to future generations.

龙泉关(墙体)

“马刨泉”畔忆六郎　“挂甲树”下思忠魂

米冬冬　贾祎玮　赵玥　刘炎羽

登临阜平明长城的长城岭口，亟待整修、以山为墙的关隘和历经400多年岁月洗礼的长城墙体，让人徒增苍凉险峻之感。

据新《阜平县志》的主编高明乡介绍，长城岭口一带自古为兵家必争之地，历史上著名的宋辽边关之战、晋奉军阀大战、清朝光绪年间的龙泉关都司秀昆抗击八国联军战事均发生在这里。特别是宋朝时，由于幽云十六州控制在辽国手中，此地成为宋辽边界。无数的戍边将士在这里留下忠勇卫国的印记，宋朝杨家将抗辽保国的故事在这里广为传颂。如阜平的养马楼、马圈沟、马沟、马坊、计马石村，古北岳恒山上的跑马梁、饮马池、辽道背，曲阳至今尚在流淌的孟良河，唐县的倒马关、歇马村，涞源的插箭岭、走马驿、马庄，易县的六郎石等，周边带“马”或“六郎”等字的地名、遗迹不胜枚举。

高明乡分析说，地名是历史的活化石。这些带“马”或“六郎”等字的地名，可以印证这里曾是宋辽边关交战之地，所以阜平县境内的长城历史并非始于明朝，在宋朝，长城岭口一带就是一道边界防线。

马跑泉

跑马梁

从冀晋交界处的长城岭沿蜿蜒的盘山公路驶向阜平龙泉关的路上，记者一行驻足在当地百姓口口相传的“马刨泉”（又名“马跑泉”）边。据说这眼高山上的泉水是杨六郎的白骏马刨出来的。为保护泉水不受污染，后人在泉眼上修筑了石房子。打开房门，沿阶而下，便有清澈甘冽的泉水沁人心脾。

马刨泉位于山西清河与河北北流河的分水岭之上，海拔1520米，周边风光怡人。据《阜平山水风物志》记载，宋朝初年，杨六郎曾驻守雁门关、偏头关、宁武关。一次，他率将与辽兵大战数日，不分胜负。双方累得人困马乏，约定各自退兵，来日再战。杨六郎策马来到长城岭下，又饥又渴，想找口水喝。仰首环顾群山四壁，一滴水也找不到。左右为难之际，陪其征战沙场多年的骏马一声长啸，前蹄猛然一举，伴随落地之声，蹄下遂现一汪清水，积水成泉。杨六郎饮过马刨清泉后精神抖擞，跨上骏马再战辽兵，不日大胜。

与杨家将有关的小说、戏曲、评书等广泛流传，宋朝名将杨六郎在我国是家喻户晓的人物。阜平与杨六郎有关的传说不止“马刨泉”。据《徐霞客游记》记载：“岭之上，巍楼雄峙，即龙泉上关也。关内古松一株，枝耸叶茂，干云俊物。”文中的古松即为当地人所说的杨六郎的“挂甲树”。长城岭上这棵古老粗大的松树为唐松。一次，宋将杨六郎与辽国交战陷入胶着之际，退到这棵松树之下，卸掉全身战甲挂在树上。后人为颂扬杨六郎的忠勇精神，称此树为“挂甲松”或“挂甲树”，并赋诗云：“将军忠义宋干城，挂甲犹传百世名。石壁云封迷鸟道，虬枝风劲听龙鸣。雄心自井兰山古，轶事偏贻草木荣。感慨示衣树上客，杨郎吾欲配颜卿。”可惜“挂甲树”在乾隆十三年（1748）时被大风吹断枯死。而马刨的清泉，汩汩缓流，常年不断，滋养着一代代阜平人和南来北往的过客。

时至今日，杨六郎英勇善战、作风简朴、号令严明、与士卒

辽道背

同甘共苦、每战都身先士卒的忠勇卫国精神，仍为国人深深敬仰和传颂。

延伸阅读：

据《宋史》记载，杨延昭生于958年，他出生两年后赵匡胤才建立北宋。杨延昭18岁时，宋辽交战，他随父出征，在朔州城下虽被乱箭射穿手臂，却越战越勇。999年隆冬，杨延昭在遂城一战成名，水浇城墙冻成坚冰，迫使南下的辽军撤退。

咸平四年（1001），杨延昭在羊山埋伏精兵大败辽军，被加封为莫州团练使。澶渊之盟后，杨延昭因戍边有功，屡次升迁。景德二年（1005），杨延昭晋升为保州防御使，不久调任高阳关副都部署。1014年，杨延昭病逝于任上，终年57岁。

杨延昭镇守边防20余年，英勇善战，震慑辽军。辽国人认为北斗七星中的第六颗主镇幽燕北方，是他们的克星。辽国人将杨延昭看作是天上的六郎星宿下凡，故称其为“杨六郎”。

Recollecting Yang Liulang on the Edge of "Mapao Spring" Reminiscing the Loyal Soul under the "Guajia Tree"

Mi Dongdong Jia Yiwei Zhao Yue Liu Yanyu

At the Changchengling(Great Wall Ridge)Pass of the Ming Dynasty in Fuping , the renovation-needed pass walled with mountains, together with the ramparts through 400 years of trials and hardships, create a desolate and dangerous atmosphere.

As Gaoming Xiang, editor-in-chief of the new *Fuping County Chronicles*, introduced, the Lingkou area of the Great Wall has been a hotly contested spot for strategic commanders since ancient times, and quite a few famous battles happened here, including Song-Liao Border Pass Battle, Jin-Feng Warlords War, and the battle between the Qing army led by Xiu Kun and the Eight-Nation Allied Forces at Longquanguan during the reign of Emperor Guangxu in the Qing Dynasty. In particular, during the Song Dynasty, because the "Sixteen You-Yun Prefectures" were controlled by the Liao State, this place became the boundary between Song and Liao. Countless frontier soldiers defended the country here with loyalty, and the story of the Yang family in the Song Dynasty resisting Liao to safeguard the country is widely spread here. There are countless places and relics with the characters "ma(horse)" and "Liu Lang" in the surrounding area. For example, Yangma Building, Majuan Gou, Ma Fang, Jimashi Village, and Paoma Liang, Yinmachi, Madaobei on the Hengshan Mountain, the Mengliang River still flowing in Quyang, and Daomaguan and Xiema Village in Tangxian County, Chajianling, Zoumayi, and Mazhuang in Laiyuan, Liulang Stone in Yixian County.

Gao Mingxiang analyzed that place names are the living fossils of history. These place names with the word "ma" and the names of generals in the Yang family can confirm that this was the place where the Song and Liao armies fought. Therefore, the history of the Fuping Great Wall did not originate from the Ming Dynasty, and it was just a borderline of defense in the Lingkou area of the Great Wall in the Song Dynasty.

On the way from Changchengling at the Shanxi-Hebei junction to Longquanguan in Fuping along the winding road, the journalists stopped by the "Mapao(Horse Digging)Spring", also known as "Mapao(Horse Running)Spring", which is widely spread among the local people. It is said that the spring water on the high mountain was dug out by the white horse of Yang Yanzhao, a famous general in the Northern Song Dynasty. To protect the spring water from pollution, later generations built a stone house on the spring. Opening the door and walking down the steps, you can smell a refreshing scent from the clear and sweet spring water.

Mapao Spring is located on the watershed between the Qinghe River in Shanxi and the Beiliu River in Hebei, with an altitude of 1,520 meters and beautiful scenery. As recorded in *Fuping Landscape and Nature Records*, in the early Song Dynasty, Yang Yanzhao(called Yang Liulang by the people) once stationed the Three Passes, namely Yanmenguan, Piantouguan and Ningwuguan. One time, he led a battle with the Liao army for several days, nip and tuck. The two sides were tired to such a degree that they both agreed to retreat and fight again the next day. Yang Liulang rode his horse to the foot of the Great Wall, hungry and thirsty, but failed to find water after looking up at the mountain. When he felt desperate, the horse that had accompanied him on the battlefield for many years roared, and its front hooves made a sudden upward move. With the sound of landing, a puddle of clear water appeared under its hooves, and the water converged into a spring. After drinking the water of the spring, Yang Liulang was fully energized, and he stepped on the steed, fought the Liao soldiers again, and soon won the battle.

The novels, operas and storytelling of The Yang Warrior Family's Saga are widely circulated, and Yang Liulang, a famous Song Dynasty general is a well-known name in our country. There are more legends in Fuping related to Yang Liulang than Mapao Spring. As recorded in *The Travels of Xu Xiake*, "on the top of the ridge lies the towering building, that is, Upper Longquanguan. An ancient pine stands within the pass, with lush leaves and luxuriant branches." This ancient pine in the book is Yang Liulang's "Guajia(hanging helmet and armour)Tree" in the local legend. This ancient big pine tree on Chajianling Ridge was planted in the Tang Dynasty. In a battle, the Song general Yang Liulang got in a stalemate with Liao, and retreated under this pine tree, where he took off his armor and hung it on the tree. To praise Yang's loyalty and courage, later generations called this tree "Guajia Pine" or "Guajia Tree" and wrote a poem for him, "General Yang is a loyal general in the Song Dynasty, and this old tree where he once hung his armor witnessed his illustrious name for generations. Clouds and mist hovering over Cliffs covered the steep path that only birds can pass, and the branches twisting like a dragon made weird noises swaying in the strong wind. His great ideals and ambitions are as majestic as long-standing Longquanguan and Taihang Mountains, and his accomplishments made all the plants and trees full of vitality. I emotionally said that Yang Yanzhao's contribution to the country is comparable to Yan Gaoqing, a loyal and righteous general of the Tang Dynasty!" It is a pity that the "Guajia Tree" was blown to death by strong winds in the thirteenth year of Qianlong(1748), while the refreshing Mapao Spring is still flowing slowly and continuously throughout the year, nourishing generations of Fuping people and travelers from all over the world.

Today, Yang Yanzhao's bravery and skillfulness in battles, simple lifestyle, strict commands and orders, willingness to share joys and sorrows with soldiers, and the heroic spirit of defending the country as the first soldier in every battle are still deeply admired and praised by the countrymen.

Extended reading:

As recorded in Song History, Yang Yanzhao was born in 958 AD, and the Northern Song Dynasty was established two years later by Zhao Kuangyin. At the age of 18, Yang Yanzhao went with his father to the Song-Liao battlefield, and was shot through his arm by arrows in Shuozhou City, but he got increasingly courageous. In the midwinter of 999 AD, Yang Yanzhao became famous in the battle of Suicheng. He ordered to freeze the city wall by pouring water onto it, forcing the Liao army to retreat southward.

In the fourth year of Emperor Xianping(1001), Yang Yanzhao ambushed crack troops in Yangshan and defeated the Liao army, and thus he was ennobled a military training officer of the Mozhou regiment. After the Chanyuan League(the peace treaty between the Northern Song Dynasty and the Liao Dynasty in 1019), Yang Yanzhao was promoted many times because of his contributions in defending the border. In the second year of Emperor Jingde(1005), Yang Yanzhao was promoted to Baozhou Defense Envoy, and soon to Deputy Capital Deployer at Gaoyangguan. In 1014, Yang Yanzhao died of illness at the age of 57.

Yang Yanzhao defended the border for more than 20 years, courageous and skillful in battle, deterring the Liao army. The Liao people believed that the sixth star of the Big Dipper dominated You-Yan in the north, and it was their nemesis. The Liao people regarded Yang Yanzhao as the sixth star, so they called him "Yang Liulang".

招提寺的红色记忆

米冬冬　贾祎玮　李娜　刘炎羽　李玉亮

“我站在一座破旧的庙宇里，站在一个二尺高的没有表情的神像面前做手术，如同在有自来水、电灯等现代化设备条件下一样地工作。过去的生活曾经引诱过我，但是为了我的理想，那些日子就让它一去不复返吧！”白求恩在给加拿大朋友的信中这样写道。

“白求恩说的庙宇就是招提寺。”新《阜平县志》的主编高明乡，在他一本本记载阜平历史的资料中，找出一张发黄的信纸，小心翼翼地展开，“我找到了当年白求恩的司药写下的回忆，其中提到白求恩大夫曾在阜平县招提寺内为晋察冀边区伤员做手术的事。”

记者一行来到高明乡的家，听他讲述发生在阜平长城岭周边的红色故事。

始建于明朝初年的招提寺，位于阜平县龙泉关镇顾家台村，距离县城34公里，驾车沿337国道向西经印钞石村、龙宿庵、马刨泉行驶14.6公里即到长城岭。据史料记载，招提寺占地6亩，有3座大殿，另有禅房、僧舍等100多间房舍。清朝时期，康熙和乾隆

招提寺大殿

招提寺

拜谒五台山，过龙泉关时曾在此寺驻跸。

抗日战争期间，招提寺先后成为晋察冀边区医院及边区政府的办公场所。1937年11月7日，根据中共中央、八路军总部的命令，晋察冀军区成立。这是共产党领导的八路军在敌后创建的第一块根据地。晋察冀边区政府、晋察冀军区司令部便在阜平县境内。

据高明乡介绍，白求恩的司药张业胜毕业于晋察冀白求恩卫生学校，后曾任北京军区总医院副院长。1998年，张业胜专门给负责编撰《阜平县志》的人写来亲笔信：1938年1月，晋察冀军区医院设有三个所（卫生所），其中第一所在河北阜平县龙泉关招提寺内，工作人员有60人，伤员有80余人。1938年8月16日—25日，白求恩大夫曾在这里为75名伤者进行了检查和手术。

白求恩在写给加拿大朋友的信中所提到的在破旧的庙宇中做手术的事，说的就是这段历史。当时十大队（相当于团的编制）队长朱良新在唐县战斗中负重伤，被民兵用担架送到招提寺一所，白求恩于1938年8月20日为其做手术，亲自护理，日夜抢救，但朱良新终因伤势过重，不幸牺牲。

1938年10月—1939年4月，晋察冀边区政府曾在招提寺和顾家台村办公。为了解决部分干部脱离群众、不坚守岗位的问题，晋察冀边区政府行政委员会主任宋劭文在招提寺发布了《边区干部"三大任务、六大纪律"》。宋劭文曾住在顾家台村王柱国家，王柱国家的墙上写着边区干部"三大任务、六大纪律"的内容。其中，"三大任务"即进行群众游击战争、配合抗日部队、维护地方秩序；"六大纪律"为：第一，服从上级命令；第二，听号令要集合；第三，外出要请假；第四，战时不逃跑；第五，盘查要仔细；第六，自己……"由于风雨侵蚀，年代比较久远，第六条纪律后面的字迹实在看不清楚了。现在这面墙也没有保留下来。"高明乡遗憾地说。

新中国成立后，招提寺又肩负起新使命：从20世纪50年代开始，它成为龙泉关镇的中小学校的校址。经过战火的洗礼，寺院已不复当年的繁盛，朗朗的读书声替代了悠扬的钟鸣声。老区条件艰苦，孩子们每天要很早从家出发，翻山越岭来到招提寺学校上课。

2012年12月29日—30日，习近平总书记来到阜平县顾家台村，看望慰问困难群众，并叮嘱："要把下一代的教育工作做好，特别是要注重山区贫困地区下一代的成长。"自此，革命老区阜平县的脱贫攻坚步伐加快，教育也逐步发力。据龙泉关镇干部马吉军介绍："龙泉关近两年的变化可大了。2016年龙泉关中心学校建成，新校址距离招提寺不到一公里，学校设施是县里最好的，有食堂，能住宿，孩子们再也不用起早贪黑跑着上学了。现在这所学校还成了保定市保师附校的龙泉关分校。"

如今，招提寺的主要建筑只剩下大门和主殿，青砖灰瓦和暗红色的木门显得凝重而沉稳。马吉军说："招提寺现在已被保护起来，乾隆帝御笔石碑也保存在镇政府，相关部门正在研究它的维修方案。龙泉关镇正在以顾家台村、骆驼湾村为中心，打造'生态长城岭，文化龙泉关'红色旅游项目，招提寺也涵盖其中。"

巍巍长城岭，莽莽龙泉关。屹立数百年的招提寺承担过红色抗战使命，培养过一代代阜平学子。在国家扶贫攻坚和美丽乡村建设的大背景下，阜平招提寺将担负起新的历史使命。

Red Memories of the Zhaoti Temple

Mi Dongdong Jia Yiwei Li Na Liu Yanyu Li Yuliang

"I stood in a dilapidated temple, and did operation in front of an expressionless Buddha of about two feet tall, just as I worked in a room equipped with modern equipments such as running water and electric lights. The past life seduced me, but for my ambition, just let those days go forever!" This is what Bethune wrote in a letter to his Canadian friend.

"The temple Bethune spoke of is Zhaoti Temple." Gao Mingxiang, editor-in-chief of the new *Fuping County Chronicles*, found a piece of yellow paper in one of his records of Fuping's history, and then unfolded it cautiously. "I found the memoirs written by Bethune's pharmacist, mentioning that Dr. Bethune had operated on the wounded soldiers in the Jin-Cha-Ji(Shanxi-Chahar-Hebei)Border Region in Zhaoti Temple of Fuping County."

A group of journalists went to Gao Mingxiang's home and listened to him telling stories about Changchengling(the Great Wall Ridge)in Fuping County.

The Zhaoti Temple, built in the early Ming Dynasty, is located in Gujiatai Village, Longquanguan Town in Fuping County. It is 34 kilometers away from the county. You can drive along the 337 National Highway westward and go through Yinchaoshi Village, Longsu'an and Mapao Spring, which are 14.6 kilometers from the Great Wall Ridge. According to historical records, Zhaoti Temple covers an area of 6 mu with three main halls. Furthermore, there are more than 100 rooms such as meditation chambers and monk's houses. During the Qing Dynasty, Emperor Kangxi and Qianlong visited Wutai Mountain and stayed in the temple when they passed Longquanguan.

During the Anti-Japanese War, Zhaoti Temple became the office of Jin-Cha-Ji Border Region Government and Border Region Hospital. On November 7th in 1937, the Central Committee of the Communist Party of China(CPC)and the Central Military Commission announced that the Jin-Cha-Ji Military Region was established, with Fuping and Wutai as the center. This was the first military base created by the Eighth Route Army led by CPC behind the enemy lines. The Jin-Cha-Ji Border Region Government and the Jin-Cha-Ji Military Region Headquarter were located in Fuping County.

According to Gao Mingxiang, this precious letter was written by Zhang Yesheng, the pharmacist of Bethune. Zhang Yesheng graduated from Bethune Health School in Jin-Cha-Ji Border Region, and later served as deputy president of General Hospital of Beijing Military Region. In 1998, Zhang Yesheng wrote a letter to the person in charge of compiling Fuping County Chronicles: in January 1938, there were three clinics in Jin-Cha-Ji Military Region Hospital, among which the first was in the Zhaoti Temple at Longquanguan of Fuping County, Hebei Province. There were 60 staff members and more than 80 wounded people. From August 16th to 25th, 1938, Dr. Bethune examined and performed surgery on 75 injured people here.

The operation mentioned by Bethune in his letter exactly happened here. Then, Zhu Liangxin, Commander of the 10th Battalion(equivalent to "regiment"), was seriously wounded in a battle in Tangxian County and was sent to the Zhaoti Temple by militias on a stretcher. Bethune operated on him on August 20, 1937. He carried out nursing and rescue personally day and night. Unfortunately, Zhu Liangxin died due to severe injury.

From October 1938 to April 1939, the office of Jin-Cha-Ji Border Region government was located in Zhaoti Temple and Gujiatai Village. In order to solve the problem that some cadres alienated themselves from the masses and did not stick to their posts, Song Shaowen, director of the administrative committee of jin-Cha-Ji Border Region Government, issued the "Three Major Tasks and Six Disciplines for Border Region Cadres" in the Zhaoti Temple.

Song Shaowen once lived in Wang Zhuguo's home in Gujiatai Village, and the content of "three major tasks and six disciplines" were written on the wall of his house. The three major tasks include conducting mass guerrilla warfare, cooperating with anti-Japanese forces, and maintaining local order; The six main disciplines include: first, obey orders from superiors; second, gather at the command; third, ask for leave when going out; fourth, never flee during the war; fifth, be careful in investigation; sixth, ... "Due to the wind and rain erosion for many years, the writings of the sixth discipline is illegible. Now that wall was not there." Gao Mingxiang said regretfully.

After the founding of People's Republic of China, the Zhaoti Temple took on a new mission, that is, since the 1950s, it has become the site of a primary and secondary school in Longquanguan Town. After the war, the temple is not as prosperous as it was before, and the sound of reading replaces the melodious bells. Due to the difficult condition in the old area, children had to set off from home very early every day and tramp over hill and dale to the Zhaoti Temple School for classes.

On December 29th and 30th, 2012, General Secretary Xi Jinping went to Gujiatai Village of Fuping County to visit impoverished families, and expressed his concerns, "We must do well in educating the next generation, and pay special attention to the growth of the next generation in impoverished mountainous areas." Since then, the pace of poverty alleviation has been accelerated and the quality of education has gradually been improved in Fuping County, an old revolutionary base area. According to Ma Jijun, a cadre of Longquanguan Town, "Longquanguan has changed a lot in the past two years. The Longquanguan Central School was completed in 2016, which is less than one kilometer away from the Zhaoti Temple. The school facilities are the best in the county with canteens and dormitories, so children don't have to go to school early and back home late. Now this school has become the Longquanguan Branch School, an affiliated school of Baoding Normal College."

Today, the remnants of the main building of the Zhaoti Temple is merely the gate and the main hall, with the black bricks, gray tiles and dark red wooden doors showing great solemnity. There are cultural relics such as a stele inscribed with Emperor Qianlong's calligraphy, erected by Fang Guancheng, the Zhili governor. "The Zhaoti temple is now under protection, and that stele is preserved in the town government office, and relevant departments are studying the plan for its maintenance ," Ma said. Longquanguan Town is building the "Ecological Great Wall Ridge, Cultural Longquanguan", a red tourism project centered on Gujiatai Village and Luotuowan Village, which also covers the Zhaoti Temple.

The towering Great Wall Ridge, and the spectacular Longquanguan. The Zhaoti Temple, standing there for hundreds of years, had accomplished the mission of resisting Japanese invaders. And generations of Fuping students were cultivated in there. In the context of the national poverty alleviation and the construction of beautiful villages, the Zhaoti Temple in Fuping will be given a new historical mission.

挂甲松就在庙的旁边

扣问鲜虞　何谓“中山”

苏兰生　梁冬艳　田莉

中山城是一座久而不远的都城。

说其久，约有2500年历史了；说不远，就在唐县。

可这座都城，几十年前人们都说，它不是中山国的国都，是后燕建国的慕容城。1999年编撰的《唐县志》也是这么说的。

这就让两者至少相差了900年。

时间，就这么解开一座老而又老的古城谜底，而这座古城的今天，又是什么模样呢？2020年5月中旬的一天，记者驱车向唐县县城西北方向行驶，10多分钟后进入太行山东麓的丘陵地带。在古代，从同样的出发点启程，走过这一丘陵地带沿路的南城子、北城子、宋庄、封庄等村庄，再向西北方向行进，是从山前平原进入太行山区的一条交通要道。

中山这座神秘都城，曾雄踞丘陵之端，可谓镇太行之东足，扼通衢之咽喉。

穿过一村又一店，到了北城子村东南，看到的是中山城已荡然无存。不过，在田野的高岗地带，还留有一段长约400米的古城残墙，标示着这座老城曾经存在过。

这段残墙，就是古城东城墙的一小段。在春秋晚期，此残墙连着其他段城墙，共同构成一座有内城和外郭的都城。唐县文物保管所所长苑永涛描述了古城的大体轮廓：这座城坐北朝南，城市东北部有内城（北城），内城呈四边各长1000米的规则正方形，为王公贵族和官府的活动居住区；都城的东、西城墙向南斜向延伸，依山就势与南墙两端连接，又形成一个不规则的斜向四边形外郭（南城），为商贸、陵墓、宗庙社稷和居民、驻防区。整个都城周长约7.5公里，总面积345万平方米。

以前，这座古城为何被“张冠李戴”呢？除历史太为久远外，另一个主要原因就是历史文献记载过于零星分散，被人们忽略了。近些年，人们对古城“回头看”，才有了今天的精准分析。

翻阅史书，最早提到中山城的文献是司马迁的《史记》。《史记·赵世家》称：“（赵敬侯）十一年，魏、韩、赵共灭晋，分其地。伐中山，又战于中人。”东汉班固的《汉书·地理志》也提到中山城。之后，晋人张曜的方志专著《中山记》及《隋图经》《括地志》等也对中山城的地望、特征、名称来历及变迁有所考证。遗憾的是，《中山记》已遗失，但可从《水经注》《太平寰宇记》《路史》《水经注疏》等史料对《中山记》的引用、转载中，印证中山城的有关内容。

那么，这座古城为何叫“中山城”呢？郦道元《水经注》称：“城内有小山，在城西侧而锐上……俗以山在邑中，故亦谓之中山城。”而城中的小山叫什么呢？苑永涛说，小山叫委粟山，在历史上这座山还设有一个关口，叫委粟关。

这就是这座老城名字的来历。同时，这也佐证了，唐县就是鲜虞人东进太行山的第一个基地。

鲜虞又是何方人呢？《山海经·北山经》称："又北三百里，曰石山……鲜于之水出焉，而南流注于虖沱。"鲜于水即今源出五台山西南，流注于滹沱河的清水河。由于"虞""于"通用，鲜于水又可称"鲜虞水"，鲜虞部族名称该与鲜虞水有关，说明此部落早期曾活动于晋北地区。

鲜虞人东迁于何时呢？史学界认为，鲜虞人曾建立鲜虞国并受封西周，公元前550年前后在唐县建都。此后，"鲜虞"与"中山"并用出现在文献中。

受封，即为诸侯国。《九州要记》称："唐县，本白狄种，最为夷狄大国，梁开平三年改为中山县。"这也说明，那时鲜虞国曾一度是夷狄诸国中的大国。

建城自是傍水，中山城也不例外。历史上，唐县的治所曾在这一带。《水经注》称："以城中有唐水，因复谓之为广唐城也。"《帝王世纪》："帝尧氏始封于唐，今中山唐县是也。尧山在焉，唐水在西北入唐河。"《畿辅通志》曰："（委）粟山，唐县北十三里，唐水出中山城之西北。"由此可见，古时唐水水源非常充沛，河水终年流淌不息。但现在，这条河已经干涸无存了。

古今中外，从无遇战事之国不多。中山国存续200多年，曾3次被灭国后复国。而备战，就得建设军事防御工程。

从中山城往北，几公里处就有一道东西向的长城穿过，这就是中山长城。此条长城从顺平境内西行到唐县境内后，穿过葫芦山，再一直向西南延伸。葫芦山的南、北、西三面是山，其在山间洼地突起。现在，在山上还能看到长城遗迹。

公元前369年，中山长城开始构筑。公元前506年，中山国在唐县建都。按时间推算，此长城至少比“中山城”晚建了130多年。文献记载，当时中山国多次受晋国、魏国和赵国所扰。但史学界认为，这道长城可能主要是为防御赵国。

国强，比长城之坚更重要。至于中山国破灭，由专家审定的《唐县历史文化之光》一书认为，中山国崇尚周礼，墨守成规旧矩，忽略了与时俱进的改革，这在东周诸国中非常突出，成为最后亡国的原因之一。

长城、都城，是故国中山御外理民的遗迹。而今天，中山城南北十几公里内，南水北调中线干渠和京昆、保阜高速公路横向穿过，新添了一项项功在千秋的民心工程。

（历史文化顾问：河北大学博物馆副馆长、教授李文龙）

Tracing the Origin of Zhongshan from the History of Xianyu Tribe

Su Lansheng　Liang Dongyan　Tian Li

Zhongshan City is an old but not far capital.

It is "old" because it has a history of 2,500 years; it is "not far" because it is right in Tangxian County.

Decades ago, people said this city was not the capital of Zhongshan State, but Murong City of Later Yan State. This is even confirmed by the *Tangxian chronicles* compiled in 1999.

The gap between the two identities is at least 900 years.

Time finally uncovered the veil of this ancient city. What does this city look like today? In the Mid-May of 2020, we drove to the northwest of Tang County and after over 10 minutes, entered the hilly area at the eastern foot of Taihang Mountain. In ancient times, an important traffic artery started from the same place, passing through the villages including Nanchengzi, Beichengzi, Songzhuang and Fengzhuang along the road, and heading northeast. It used to be a strategic place stretching from the piedmont plain to Taihang Mountain area.

This mysterious capital city once stood at the end of the hills. It was described as the eastern foot of Taihang Mountain and the thoroughfare of the city.

Walking through one village after another, we finally reached the southeast of Beichengzi Village, where there is no longer any traces of an ancient city. However, in the high hills of the field, there is still a section of the

400-meter ancient city wall, indicating that the city once existed.

This remnant wall is a small section of the east wall of the ancient city. In the late Spring and Autumn Period, the remnant wall connected with other sections of the city wall, forming a capital city which comprised of an Inner City and an Outer City. Yuan Yongtao, director of the Cultural Protection Office of Tang County, described the general framework of the ancient city: the city faces south, and there is an Inner City(North City)in the northeast. The Inner City is a regular square with a length of 1,000 meters on each side, which is a living area for princes, nobles and officials. The east and east walls of the capital city extend to the south in an oblique direction, connecting with the two ends of the south wall along the mountain, forming an irregular oblique triangular Outer City(South City). The Outer City is a place for trade, mausoleums, ancestral temples, residents and garrison areas. The capital city has a circumference of about 7.5 kilometers and a total area of 3.45 million square meters.

So why was the ancient Zhongshan City mistakenly recognized in the past? Apart from the remoteness of the history, another important cause is the scattered literature records that have been largely ignored. The recent years have witnessed a "return" to the origin of the ancient city, giving rise to today's accurate explanation.

Among all historical records, the *Records of the Grand Historian* compiled by Sima Qian was the earliest one to mention Zhongshan City. *Records of the Grand Historian*: *History of Zhao Aristocratic Family* writes: "In the 11th year(of Marquis Zhaojing), Wei, Han and Zhao jointly conquered Jin and seized its land, then they raided Zhongshan and fought against its citizens". Zhongshan City was also mentioned in the *The Book of Han History*: *Geographic Records* compiled by Ban Gu in the Eastern Han Dynasty. Later, in his monographs of *Zhongshan Records*, *Classic of Sui Maps* and *Treatise Extended to All Regions*, Zhang Yao from the Jin Dynasty examined the position, characteristics, name origin and historical changes of Zhongshan City. Regrettably, the original work of *Zhongshan Records* has been missing. But the citations and restatement of the book in *The Water Classic*, *The Universal Geography of the Taiping Era*, T*he Grand History* and *Commentary on the Water Classic* can be used as evidence for information about Zhongshan City.

Then, why was the ancient city called "Zhongshan"? In his work *The Water Classic*, Li Daoyuan argued that "there was a small hill in the city...which lies steeply in the west of the city...local folks referred to it as the 'hill in the city', thus it got the name 'Zhongshan'". So what was the hill in the city called? Yuan Yongtao pointed out that the hill was actually called the Weisu Hill, where a pass named the "Weisu Pass" was once established.

This is the origin of the name of this ancient city. In the meantime, this is also a proof that Tangxian County was the first base established by the Xianyu Tribe in Taihang Mountain after they moved eastwards.

Who were the Xianyu people? In the chapter of *Classic of Mountains and Seas:North Mountain Classic*, which writes, "further 300 li(one li refers to about one third of an English mile and now has a standard length of a half -kilometer) north lies a place named Shishan... the ancient Xianyu water springs up here and flows towards 'Hutuo'(villages by the river)". The so-called Xianyu water originates from the southwest of Wutai Mountain and flows into the clean stream of the Hutuo River. In Chinese, Xianyu water has many homophonic forms in writing. The Xianyu tribe may thus be associated with Xianyu water, indicating that the tribe might have been based in northern Shanxi in their earlier times.

When did the Xianyu people relocate themselves to the east? Historians believe that the Xianyu people once founded a state and received a title from the Western Zhou Dynasty, and around 550 BC. They established a capital in today's Tangxian County. Later, terms of "Xianyu" and "Zhongshan" were used interchangeably in historical literature.

Receiving a title from the emperor meant that it was officially recognized as a vassal state. According to the *Records of the Nine Provinces*, "[people in] Tangxian County were originally decedents of the Baidi clan, the largest state of eastern and northern tribes; in the third year of Emperor Kaiping of Liang, it was renamed as Zhongshan County". This is to say that the then Xianyu State was a large state among the states of eastern and northern tribes.

Places near rivers were naturally ideal choices for capitals, and Zhongshan City was no exception. Historically, the governing territory of Tangxian County also covered this area. As recorded in *The Water Classic*, "Tang River ran across the city, thus the place is also called the Guangtang

County". *The Emperor's Time in China* writes, "the original fiefdom of Emperor Yao was Tang, that is, today's Zhongshan Tang County. During Yao's rein, the Tang Water flew towards the Tang River in the northwest". *The General History of the Capital Region* writes, "[Wei] Su Mountain lies 13 li north of Tang County, and the Tang River originates from the northwest of Zhongshan City." As such, the sources of Tang water in ancient times were plentiful and water was perennially flowing. However, it has been dried and traceless today.

In ancient and modern times, there are few states that have never encountered war. Zhongshan State existed for more than 200 years and was restored after being destroyed three times. Fortifications need to be built to prepare for war.

A few kilometers from Zhongshan City to the north, there is an east-west Great Wall passing through. This is the Zhongshan Great Wall. The Great Wall runs westward from Shunping County to Tangxian County, passes through Hulu Mountain, and then extends to the southwest. Hulu Mountain, which protrudes among mountains and valleys, are surrounded by mountains in the south, north, and west. Now, the remnants of the Great Wall can be seen on the mountain.

In 369 BC, the Zhongshan Great Wall began to be constructed. Around 500 BC, the Zhongshan State established its capital in Tangxian County. Calculated by time, the Great Wall was built at least 130 years later than"Zhongshan City". It is recorded that the Zhongshan State was repeatedly hassled by Jin, Wei and Zhao States at that time. However, the historians believe that this section of the Great Wall may be constructed mainly for defense against Zhao State.

National strength is more important than the strength of the Great Wall. As for the collapse of Zhongshan State, according to the book *The Light of History and Culture in Tang County*, which has been approved by experts, Zhongshan State advocated Zhou etiquette, adhered to the traditional rules and conventions, and neglected the reform that kept pace with the times. This eventfully resulted in the annihilation of the nation, which is widely seen among the Eastern Zhou States.

The Great Wall and the capital city are the relics of Zhongshan city, which witnessed efforts of the government to fight against enemies and govern the country. Today, within a dozen kilometers from the north to the south of Zhongshan City, the major canal in the middle route of the South-to-North Water Diversion Project, the Jingkun(Beijing-Kunming)and Baofu Expressways have crossed the city horizontally. These projects have gained mass support and achieved lasting success.

(The consultant on history and culture: Professor Li Wenlong, deputy curator of Hebei University Museum)

中山城出土文物

中山城出土文物

长城长

刘柯旋

“都说长城两边是故乡，你知道长城有多长。它一头挑起大漠边关的冷月，它一头连着华夏儿女的心房……”

保定籍已故艺术家阎肃词作《长城长》道出了长城恢宏的气势和深远的意境。

保定古长城遗存丰富，有中山长城、燕南长城、明长城。战国时期，燕昭王即位后，励精图治，招贤纳士，燕国进入最强盛时期。名将乐毅南伐强齐，秦开北破东胡，燕国开始向东北开拓。在此前后，燕国开始修筑南、北两道长城。沿南易水河而建的燕南长城，又称“易水长城”。

河北大学博物馆副馆长、教授李文龙称，燕南长城位于保定、廊坊境内的易县、徐水、容城、安新、雄县、文安、大城七县，总长约259公里。它首起易县西南太和庄西侧的狼窝尖山，沿南易水河北岸延伸，进入徐水后继续沿瀑河（南易水河下游）北岸东行至遂城西。长城跨瀑河，向东经徐水城入容城、安新，沿白洋淀北堤转北、转东而行。进入雄县后跨越大清河，沿河北岸进入廊坊市文安县。

古长城

燕南长城既是燕国的边界军事防御设施，又是防范水患的大型水利工程。据徐水区文物管理所所长商鸿果介绍，徐水境内的燕长城，是燕南长城中保存最好的。其从徐水、易县交界处至徐水遂城镇城西村，临瀑河断续残存城墙9000多米，墙体最高处17米，最宽处35米，为河北省重点文物保护单位。燕长城在战国时期为捍卫燕国南部疆土做出了重要贡献，在北宋时期不仅成为宋辽界城，还是兵家战略要地。

仲夏清晨，走在徐水瀑河乡解村瀑河西岸，隔岸便是燕长城现存的“精华”地段，长约1000米，夯土筑造。墙体高低起伏，黄土裸露，如刃如壁，饱经2300多年风霜，依旧岿然挺立。酸枣树粗壮的根扎下一两米深，纵横交错，力道强劲。瀑河沿着长城的方向一路东南，将南水北调清水送往雄安新区。

“徐水区文物管理所联合沿途乡镇、村、学校对燕长城设置宣传展示牌、文物保护标识，使其成为传统文化教育基地。一些学校在新生入学、学生毕业，以及开展主题班会时，会到城址处组织活动；一些村庄街巷、文艺团队、商业门店也以‘长城’命名，使长城文化、长城精神植根于百姓特别是青少年心中。”商鸿果说。

这是一处距瀑河水库出水闸200米的平静水面，逶迤斑驳的长城倒映水中。一尾钓竿，一顶草帽，独钓清幽。“城在河里走，鱼在墙上游，干涸30多年又见这神奇景致，可得把长城保护好，把一河清水守护好。”老人的笑声在水面荡漾。

车铃悦耳，环保志愿者骑行队十几人蓝装驶过，与车后“不让一滴污水流入白洋淀”的红角旗相映成趣。近年，徐水区深度服务雄安新区生态建设，广宣传，投巨资，整治城乡环境，进行河道修浚、防污，建成20公里长、0.5公里宽的环雄安林带，并着手建设漕河两侧2.5万亩生态廊道，打造屏障雄安的“绿色长城”。

登上燕长城，一夜暴雨冲刷后的地表依然坚实。绿草萋萋，灌木丛生，随风摇曳，似有万千铁甲镇守其中。放眼四周，红顶白墙，绿意葱茏，鸡犬相闻，水流淙淙，好似一幅甜美祥和的乡村水墨图。目光越过连绵的青纱帐，往南三四公里，徐水大王店经济开发区长城汽车园规模宏大。林木掩映中的厂房、全国自动化程度颇高的民族品牌整车生产基地、国内先进的高速环形试车跑道依稀可见。

出保定城区北延到瀑河水库止，宽阔的朝阳大街把横亘东西的燕南长城和“每天进步一点点”（长城汽车企业精神）的长城汽车园连在一起，南北相望，成为一道特殊景观。长城汽车携手10万职工，浇筑这道巍峨壮观的“产业长城”：扩大内需，布局海外，危中寻机。长城汽车“走出去”的不仅是产品，更是长城精神、中国实力。

长城文化在传承——国人对长城的了解不断深入，理解愈加丰富，情感更加厚重；长城精神在弘扬——以铁骨铮铮的中华气节、万众一心的血肉之躯，凝聚复兴力量，共筑新的长城。

“太阳照，长城长，长城雄风万古扬。你要问长城在哪里，就在咱老百姓的心坎上！”

The Long Great Wall

Liu Kexuan

"It's said that on both sides of the great wall is our hometown. Do you know how long the Great Wall is? One end of it reaches the cold moon at the border of the desert, and the other end connects the hearts of the Chinese people..."

The Long Great Wall with lyrics by the late artist Yan Su from Baoding expresses the grandeur and profound artistic conception of the Great Wall.

Baoding ancient Great Wall is rich in relics, including the Zhongshan Great Wall, the Yannan great wall and the Ming Great Wall. During the Warring States Period, after King Yan Zhao ascended the throne, he made great efforts to govern the country and recruit talents, and Yan State entered the most powerful period. Since Yue Yi, a famous general, defeated Qi State in the south, and Qin Kai conquered Donghu in the north, Yan state began to expand to the northeast. Before or after that, Yan state began to build the South and North Great Walls. The Yannan Great Wall built along the Nanyishui River is also known as "Yishui Great Wall".

Li Wenlong, deputy director of Hebei University Museum and professor, said that the Yannan Great Wall is located in seven counties of Yixian, Xushui, Rongcheng, Anxin, Xiongxian, Wen'an and Dacheng in Baoding and Langfang, with a total length of about 259 kilometers. It starts from langwojianshan on the west side of Taihezhuang in the southwest of Yixian County and extends along the north bank of the Nanyishui River. After entering Xushui County, it continues to travel eastward along the north bank of the Puhe River (downstream of the Nanyishui River) to the west of Suicheng City. The Great Wall crosses the Puhe river, goes eastward through Xushui into Rongcheng and Anxin, and then turns north and east along the north bank of the Baiyangdian Lake. After entering Xiongxian County, it crossed the Daqing River and entered Wen'an County of Langfang City along the North Bank of the river.

The Yannan Great Wall is not only the border military defense facilities of the Yan state, but also a large-scale water conservancy project to prevent floods. According to Shang Hongguo, director of the Cultural Relics Management office of Xushui District, the Yan Great Wall in Xushui is the best preserved section of the Yannan Great Wall. From the junction of Xushui and Yixian County to Chengxi Village, Suicheng Town, Xushui, the remaining rampart along the Puhe River is more than 9,000 meters long, with the highest part of 17 meters and the widest part of 35 meters. It is a key cultural relics protection unit in Hebei Province. During the Warring States Period, the Yan Great Wall made an important contribution to the defense of the southern territory of Yan State. In the Northern Song Dynasty, it became not only a Song-Liao border city, but also a strategic place for military strategists.

On a midsummer morning, walking on the west bank of the Puhe River in Xie Village of Puhe Township in Xushui District, you can see the existing "treasured" section of the Great Wall built by the State of Yan across the river, which is about 1,000 meters long and made of rammed earth. The walls undulate with bare loess, like blades or cliffs, standing straight and upright though battered by wind and frost for over 2,300 years. The thick roots of wild jujube trees spread one or two meters deep, zigzagging and intertwining strongly into the ground. Running southeastward along the Great Wall, the Puhe River takes clear water of South-to-North Water Diversion to the Xiong'an New Area.

"The Cultural Relics Management Office of Xushui District, together with towns, villages and schools along the way, set up signboards and cultural relics protection signs on the Great Wall, making it a traditional culture and education base. Some schools organize activities at the city site when new students enroll, students graduate, and theme class meetings are held. Some villages, streets, art teams, and commercial stores are also named 'the Great Wall', so that the culture and spirit of the Great Wall are rooted in the hearts of the people, especially the young people." Shang Hongguo said.

This is a stretch of still water 200 meters from the outlet gate of the Puhe Reservoir, reflecting the winding mottled Great Wall. With a rod in hand, an old man wearing a straw hat is fishing quietly. "The Great Wall runs in the river and fishes swim above the walls. I haven't seen these since the river dried up over 30 years ago. We must protect the Great Wall and the crystal-clear river well." The old man's laughter spreads on the rippling water surface.

With melodious bells, about a dozen cyclists of the voluntary environmental team in blue pass by, contrasting finely with the red pennants reading "No drop of polluted water can flow into the Baiyangdian Lake" behind the bikes. In recent years, Xushui District deepens services to the ecological construction of the Xiong'an New Area, widely publicizing and investing a huge sum into the improvement of rural and urban environment, including dredging and protecting the watercourse from pollutants, building a forest belt 20 kilometers long and 0.5 kilometer wide surrounding the Xiong'an New Area, and starting building an ecological corridor covering an area of 25,000 mu by both sides of the Caohe River, to create a "Green Great Wall" guarding the Xiong'an New Area.

Stepping on the Great Wall built by the State of Yan, you will find the ground still solid despite a storm for a whole night. In lush grass and dense bushes dancing in the wind, it seems that tens of thousands of armored warriors were in defense. Looking around, you can see red roofs and white walls, luxuriant vegetation, close neighborhoods and bubbling streams, which look like a sweet and peaceful landscape. Beyond the continuous green fields, three or four kilometers to the south is the large-scale Great Wall Motors Park in the Dawangdian Economic Development Zone of Xushui District. Through leaves of trees, workshop buildings, a national brand vehicle manufacturing base with a rather high level of automation, and an advanced circular high-speed test track are discernible.

Extending northward from downtown Baoding to the Puhe Reservoir, the broad Chaoyang Street joins the Yannan Great Wall running east and west and the Great Wall Motors Park "Improving Little by Little Every Day" (Great Wall Motors corporate culture), which look at each other and form a special landscape. Great Wall Motors with a staff of 100,000 people is building the grand spectacular "Industrial Great Wall": expanding domestic demand, laying out overseas, and finding opportunities in the crisis. Great Wall Motors "goes global" not only with products, but also with the Great Wall spirit and the strength of China.

The Great Wall culture is being inherited—The Chinese keep deepening their understanding of the Great Wall, enrich their comprehension and have deeper affection; the Great Wall spirit is being carried forward—With the dauntless and unyielding morale of the Chinese nation, and flesh and blood of all the people of one mind, we concentrate strength for revitalization and forge our new Great Wall together.

"The sun shines on the long Great Wall, the glory of which will be carried forward eternally. If you ask me where the Great Wall is, it is just in the hearts of the masses."